TEA AND EMPATHY

ALSO BY SHANNA SWENDSON

The Enchanted, Inc. Series

Enchanted, Inc.

Once Upon Stilettos

Damsel Under Stress

Don't Hex with Texas

Much Ado About Magic

No Quest for the Wicked

Kiss and Spell

Frogs and Kisses

Enchanted Ever After

Enchanted, Inc. Stories

Paint the Town Red

Criminal Enchantment

Tales of Enchantment (story collection)

The Lucky Lexie Mysteries

Interview with a Dead Editor

Case of the Curious Crystals

Mystery of the Drowned Driver

Case of the Vanishing Visitor

Secret of the Haunted Hotel

Case of the Broken Bridge

Mystery of the Secret Santa

The Rebels Series

Rebel Mechanics

Rebel Magisters

Rebels Rising

The Fairy Tale Series

A Fairy Tale

To Catch a Queen

A Kind of Magic

Twice Upon a Christmas

Make Mine Magic

Spindled

TEA AND EMPATHY

SHANNA SWENDSON

CHAPTER 1

E lwyn Howell was certain she didn't have long to live, which meant she needed to find a good place to die. Her ability to keep walking was likely to give out long before she breathed her last, and while she still had the strength to walk she felt she should use it to find a proper place to spend her final moments. If she kept going until she fell, she might find herself in a spot that was entirely unsuitable.

Not here, she thought, surveying her present surroundings. The trees were spindly, so she'd be left exposed to the sun and sky. She wanted to be able to see the sky as she died, but she didn't want to feel she was wilting under the sun. So, she kept walking.

Not here, either. This spot was too shadowy. She wouldn't be able to tell when the darkness closed in. There was no point in feeling like she was dead before she actually was.

Definitely not here. The masses of tree roots and stones would make for an uncomfortable place to lie. She didn't want to spend her final moments in misery.

This spot might do. It was shaded, but the sky was visible through the leaves, and the ground was nice and mossy. But it was on the side of the road, where anyone traveling by could see her. Her body would surely be robbed before it was even cold. They'd discover the silk shift—her one last bit of luxury from her old life—and assume that meant there would be other treasures on her, and then there was no telling what indignities her body would suffer as the robbers searched for something that didn't exist. Not that she'd be there to experience any indignities, but she didn't have to abandon her standards merely because she was dead.

That meant anywhere along the main road was simply unacceptable. She'd turn on the next byway she came across. Then she might find a private spot where she could die in comfort and remain unmolested except by the creatures of the forest. She wasn't sure why, but there seemed to be less indignity in being returned to nature by natural forces than in being pawed at by people looking to take her few remaining possessions.

She wasn't sure how much longer it took before the road crossed a lane, but she was still on her feet and moving, so it couldn't have been too long. This looked like exactly what she needed. There was no sign indicating where the lane went, and the forest was closing in on it, so it didn't appear as though anyone was bothering to keep it open. She turned and soon felt like she was being absorbed into the womb of the forest. Yes, this was more like it. She was surrounded by trees, with hardly any sign other than the track she followed that any human had ever passed this way. Birds sang, and the leaves rustled gently overhead in the breeze. It was lovely enough to make her wish she could stay longer.

She came to a low stone bridge over a brook and paused at its crest. The spot just past the bridge was exactly what she was looking for—a good mix of trees and sun, a cushion of moss, and the gentle babbling of the brook. She could stop there and allow herself to drift away.

There was just one problem: She didn't actually want to die. She had simply run out of the resources she needed to continue to live. She'd used the last of her money and had sold anything of value other than the silk shift and a necklace she didn't dare sell because it would reveal her identity and whereabouts, if she wasn't accused of being a thief merely for having it. She hadn't slept indoors for more than a month, as she prioritized buying food over having shelter. Now she could afford neither. She hadn't eaten in two days, and her body couldn't continue to function much longer. The sort of food she could forage at this time of year wouldn't do much to sustain her, and she didn't have the skills or strength to do odd jobs that might earn a crust of bread or piece of cheese.

No, that wasn't entirely true. She did have skills, valuable ones that had not only earned her bread, but also a suite of rooms in a palace and luxurious furnishings. At the very least, she could earn meals and shelter, but she didn't dare use those skills. She didn't trust them anymore, and even if she tried, they might draw attention that could lead to her being arrested for murder, and she still wasn't certain that she wasn't guilty. Not that it mattered, since the people who would rule on her fate had already decided.

So, should she stop and give up at this perfect spot or keep going and risk falling in an entirely unsuitable place— or perhaps find a way to survive? A bridge like this meant there must be some sort of civilization ahead, and maybe she could stoop to begging. She hadn't sunk that low yet. It might buy her more time, but would that merely be prolonging the inevitable? Without actually consciously deciding, she resumed walking down the lane.

When she rounded a curve in the lane, she emerged from the tunnel of trees and gasped at the sight that unfolded ahead of her. Hills formed a cup-like valley, and in that valley nestled a village. Cottages built from honey-colored stone lined the sides of the lane, the late-afternoon sun casting the whole scene with a golden glow. It drew her in; even without realizing, she walked more briskly, eager to reach the village.

The first cottage she passed, on the very edge of the woods, took her back to her youth, where she'd begun her training. It was a two-story cottage of golden stone with mullioned front windows and a tall thatched roof with dormer windows emerging from it. It stood just far enough back from the road to have a front garden that was a wild riot of plants, completely untamed. The cottage itself appeared to be sound, but she couldn't imagine anyone would live there and leave the garden that untended. They'd have to fight their way through the overgrown shrubbery down the front walk to reach the door. Every fiber of her being called out to her to tend to that garden, but she forced herself to keep going.

The next row of cottages she passed after crossing a bridge snuggled together, and soon she was in the village proper, with unbroken lines of cottages lining both sides of the lane. She didn't see another person. Was the village abandoned—or worse? Vines ran amok, almost entirely covering some of the buildings. Some of the windows were broken, if they still had glass, and some looked like open wounds. Shutters sagged on hinges, with peeling paint.

Where there were plants and flowers, they were overgrown, coming out into the lane. She was beginning to think that the village had been abandoned for years when she saw lights in a window ahead, the warm glow and flicker of fire and candlelight speaking of home and comfort. The sight tugged at her heart, filling her with a longing so strong it made her want to weep.

The lane led to a triangular market area in the heart of the village, with the lane veering toward the right and a smaller lane peeling off to the left. She assumed that lane wound its way up the hill toward the castle that loomed over the village. She could see a couple of turrets and chimneypots peeking above the trees at the top of the hill. She was still the only person out and about, which felt eerie. She shivered and wrapped her shawl more tightly around her shoulders.

A building that looked like an inn stood across the market from her, but no lights shone in its windows. Not that she had the money for a room or a meal. There was a bakery, but its windows were shuttered. Its sign was freshly painted, so it appeared to be in operation, but no light came from the window above it, so she couldn't knock and ask for any day-old bread. She walked around a little more, trying to work up the nerve to knock on the door at one of the homes with light showing through the windows and beg for food.

A glimpse of herself in a dark window changed her mind. She looked utterly terrifying. She'd slam the door in her own face, so she couldn't blame anyone else for doing so. She was filthy and ragged. Perhaps if she could find a place to rest and wash up, in the morning she could approach the townspeople.

That cottage, she thought. If it was truly abandoned, she could rest there, out of the elements. It stood on the shore of the brook, so she'd be able to get water to wash, and there might be something edible in that overgrown garden. She turned and headed back the way she'd come.

When she reached the cottage, the front door stood ajar. It hadn't been open when she'd passed earlier, had it? Or had she merely not noticed the door behind the wild garden? Curious, she opened the gate and made her way down the front walk, pushing aside the overgrown plants. They weren't fully leafed out yet, but they hadn't been cut back the previous winter, so it was mostly a tangle of dead stalks and vines, with small bits of green peeking from underneath.

At the door, she knocked and called out. The door swung fully open at her knock, but there was no response to her call. The front room was empty. She stepped inside and saw a counter at the far left corner with shelves behind it. This must have been a shop of some kind. A small table with two wooden chairs by it sat in front of the window near the counter. The tops of the walls had been painted with a border of vines and flowers, with the occasional heart. Although the room appeared abandoned, it was immaculate, without a speck of dust. The windowpanes were crystal clear and there wasn't a cobweb in sight. Perhaps the business was no longer in operation but someone still lived in the cottage.

Which meant she shouldn't intrude. She was turning to leave when she saw that the door at the rear of the front room also stood ajar, which she could have sworn wasn't the case when she first entered. She must not have noticed. She knocked on the door and called out again. Again, there was no response. Her knock pushed the door open into a hallway. A doorway on one side of the hallway revealed a room that must have served as a parlor or sitting room, though it held only a chair and a small table that were situated in front of the cold fireplace. Bookcases lined the walls of the room, but they held only a couple of books. There were lace curtains at the window, and more of that decorative painting circled the tops of the walls. More hearts and flowers had been painted on the ceiling, and the rug in front of the chair was in shades of rose and pink, matching the painted hearts and flowers.

On the other side of the hall was a kitchen that took her straight back to her childhood. It was exactly like Mother Alis's kitchen in her cottage, with a great hearth, a bread oven set into the wall beside it, and a heavy table in the middle of the room. The only difference was the pump at the sink—a real luxury. She could almost smell the bread baking and the herbal preparations brewing as she traveled back in her memory. Perhaps none of her woes would have occurred if she'd been satisfied with that simple life, if she'd never left the cottage in the woods.

But no, Mother Alis had been the one to send her away, saying there was far more good she could do with her talents elsewhere. Leaving hadn't been her decision. But she had later chosen a different kind of life than a humble cottage.

The aroma of something cooking wasn't entirely in her memory, she realized. It wasn't bread she smelled. It was something stewing in the pot hanging on the hook over the fire. Someone was here, after all. She turned and hurried toward the front door, hoping she could get away before the cottage's residents noticed her presence. It was hard to leave that cozy kitchen and cooking food, but explaining her trespass would be even worse.

The door to the front room slammed shut before she could reach it. Elwyn understood then, and panic rose within her. This cottage didn't just remind her of her youth. It was another of the same kind. That meant this was the last place Elwyn wanted to be. This was worse than being caught by the residents.

She raced down the hall to the back door, but she couldn't get it to open. "Let me out of here!" she demanded as she pulled on the doorknob. "I'm not what you think I am. I can't be. I don't belong here."

The scent of the stew came wafting out of the kitchen toward her, making her stomach growl.

"That's not fair," she said, sagging wearily against the door. The truth was, she didn't have it in her to go anywhere else, even if she could get out of the cottage. There was food here, and she was clearly wanted, if not a prisoner. "Very well," she said with a sigh. "One night." A meal and a night's sleep under a roof, and then she could see about finding someplace more suitable or moving on. She couldn't stay, since a cottage like this came with obligations she couldn't fulfill.

Resigned, she returned to the kitchen and set her bag down. She went to check the stew, but the spoon moved away from her. "Very well," she said. "I'll leave it to you. I'll explore." Mother Alis had had such a helper, and it was equally territorial about cooking.

She went back out to the hallway and found the door to the staircase. The stairs were steep and narrow, but there was a window at the top of the stairs that lit the way with the glow of the setting sun. There were two spacious rooms on the upper floor. One held a jumble of furniture and other objects, but the other held a bed dressed with what appeared to be fresh linens. She could smell a hint of lavender. Lace curtains hung at the windows, and still more floral designs had been painted on the walls. No clothes hung on the hooks on the wall and the chest at the foot of the bed held only a few linens. If anyone lived in this house, they had fewer possessions than she had, aside from the house itself and the furniture. The house's helper must have been in desperate need of company. No wonder it didn't want to let her go.

When she got back downstairs, she went to the back door and said, "I'm not fleeing. I give you my word. I just want to look at the garden. I might be able to bring in some herbs or greens." She gestured toward her bag in the kitchen, "I'm leaving everything I own. I won't go anywhere without my belongings." After a long pause, the door opened, and she stepped out to find the garden of her dreams. Like the front garden, it had been badly neglected, with parts of it dead and other parts overgrown. If the helper was like the one at Mother Alis's cottage, its powers were limited to the house itself. The brook ran alongside one side of the garden. There was a well, a large shed, and a privy behind it. A small orchard filled the back of the garden.

She availed herself of the privy, where she was fully convinced that no one had lived in this house in a very long time, as there was no odor at all. The shed turned out to be a workroom. Bundles of dried herbs hung from the rafters, and there were plenty of empty bottles and jars. Without the helper to keep things tidy, the shed was dusty and filled with cobwebs. Elwyn took some dried thyme and rosemary from the hanging bunches to help season the stew, and she found some parsley and a few young leaves of greens on her way back to the cottage that she thought would make a nice salad.

Back in the cottage, she left her bounty on the kitchen table, but before she could move to prepare a salad, a brisk wind rose to nudge her out of the kitchen and across the hall. There she found that the fire in the sitting room had been lit and a tub sat in front of the fire, steam rising from it. A few dried flower petals floated on top of the water. She got the hint that she needed to wash before dinner. She had to agree. She was filthy from the road and probably smelled terrible. She peeled off her clothes, stepped into the tub, and sank under the water, letting it cover her hair. When she couldn't hold her breath any longer, she emerged, leaving only her head above the water.

She scrubbed her hair and body with the soap that had been left by the tub. It was an old, dry bar, but it smelled of lavender. The former resident of this house must have made it. She wondered again what had happened to that person—to this village. It didn't look like there had been any sort of natural disaster. The buildings were all intact, if somewhat neglected. A plague, perhaps? But the lack of belongings in the house suggested that someone had moved out and taken everything that could be easily moved. If the resident had died and her belongings had been looted, the house would probably look different, unless the helper had tidied up in the aftermath. But she doubted the helper would have abided the looting.

When her skin began to shrivel, she reluctantly emerged from the bath and dried herself on the soft towel that had been left beside the tub. Then she discovered that her clothes had been cleaned and laid out on the chair. Her prized silk shift was white once more, and it was sheer heaven to slide it over her newly cleaned body. Her woolen dress smelled fresh.

She took the wooden comb from her pack and combed the snarls out of her wet hair, leaving it loose to dry. Instead of putting on her stockings and boots, she took the pair of cloth slippers from her pack and put them on.

Feeling like a new woman, she left the sitting room and crossed the hall to the kitchen, where the table had been set as though for an honored guest. A cloth had been laid, and candles on tall stands burned in the middle of the table. Places had been set at either end of the table, with bowls, plates, cutlery, and cups, though only one of the bowls had been filled with stew. A sprig of parsley garnished the stew, and a salad had been arranged on a plate. "This looks wonderful," she said to the invisible helper as the chair in front of the bowl scooted out for her. She took a seat and wondered if she should wait. The helper had apparently set a place for itself, even if it wasn't going to actually eat. When the spoon at the other setting rose, she took that as her cue.

It took all her self-control not to wolf down the stew like a starving animal, although that's what she was. Not only did she not want to appear rude, but she knew that her empty stomach would rebel if she filled it too full or too quickly. She took careful spoonfuls, forcing herself to chew thoroughly. The lentils must have been old because they were chewier than they should have been, but she knew the helper had done as well as it could with what was available in the house. "Mmm, delicious," she said. The cup across the table rose, as if in a toast. She raised her own in response.

Maybe by providing an evening of companionship, she could persuade the helper to let her leave. Then again, it wouldn't be so bad to rest awhile before resuming her journey. If she did, she'd need to find more food, but she had no means for buying more food. With a sigh, she realized that she might have a night or two of comfort here, but her problems hadn't been solved. She wasn't going to die immediately, but she still didn't know how she was going to live.

CHAPTER 2

W hen Elwyn first woke, she wasn't entirely sure
where she was. She was warm and comfortable
and not hungry. It was just the way things had been when
she was living in the palace. Was she still in the palace? Had
all the wandering, hiding, and starving merely been a
terrible nightmare?

She refused to open her eyes for several minutes,
clinging to the hope that she would be back in her chambers and all would be right. But then she noticed how sore
her feet and legs were and the way her back and shoulders
ached from carrying a pack. The sheets she lay on, although
crisp and clean, weren't quite as fine as those she remembered. She couldn't possibly still be in her old life.
Cautiously, she opened her eyes to see sun streaming into
an attic room with lace curtains billowing in a breeze and
roses and hearts stenciled on the walls.

She couldn't help but sigh at the proof that it had all
been real. On the other hand, she was safe for the moment
and had experienced the best night of sleep she'd had in

months. There was a very good chance she'd have something to eat for breakfast. She was also possibly being held prisoner by a magical entity that wanted her to serve as a healer, but she'd worry about that later. She dressed and headed downstairs to find the table set once more, though this time without the cloth, and a bowl of porridge waiting for her. There was no milk or cream, but it had honey drizzled over it and it was better than anything she'd had in ages. She'd been lucky to eat anything at all most mornings.

"This is good," she told the invisible helper. "I appreciate your hospitality, but I shouldn't impose on you for too long. I'm afraid I can't stay here. I know you're looking for a new healer to take residence, but believe me, you don't want me."

A cup full of hot liquid slid across the table toward her. She sniffed and realized it was tea—real tea, not an herbal tisane. "Oh, I haven't had this in so long," she said after taking a sip. "But I still can't stay."

A jar flew off a shelf to land in front of her. It was empty, but it had been labeled as a salve for treating bruises. "I can't do that anymore," she insisted. "I'm no healer. And it doesn't look as though there are enough people in the village to support one." She took another sip of tea, savoring the flavor before swallowing it. "I can read and write, do sums, and know a great deal about the natural world, so I suppose I could teach school." She glanced down at her ragged clothes. "But I can't imagine anyone being willing to hire me. I have no references. I'm sure I'd make an excellent governess, but if I showed up at the sort of home where they'd want to hire a governess, they'd have me turned away as a beggar." She gave a bitter laugh. "It seems you need a certain amount of money in order to be suited to earn money. There's only so far mending can go to make a person presentable."

Another jar flew off the shelf and landed in front of her. It contained dried flowers, and the label said it was elder. Good for treating coughs and congestion, she thought automatically. "I'm feeling just fine," she said. "No cough at all. And if I start dispensing things like this, word will get out that there's a healer here, and then the people who are looking for me will find me. I wasn't a very good healer, anyway. I let a patient die of a simple wound that should have been barely an inconvenience."

There was no response for a moment, and then a small vial of dark glass landed on the table in front of her. The label said it was essence of crabapple. Elwyn was skeptical about the power of floral essences, though some healers swore by them, and she'd memorized their alleged properties during her training. "So you think I need to heal my sense of unworthiness?" she said wryly. She was in bad shape if an invisible spirit was diagnosing her, though if it was like the spirit in the cottage where she'd trained, it was the spirit of the first healer to occupy the cottage, combined with those of other healers who'd died there and joined the spirit of the cottage, so the healer probably knew more than she did. "Maybe I am unworthy." A glass of water landed next to the bottle. She unstoppered the bottle and dripped a few drops into the water. "I'm not sure how potent it will be after all this time," she said before drinking the water. She felt a slight tingle spread through her whole body. Whoever had made that tincture had a real gift. She actually felt slightly better about herself, though she suspected it was more to do with the magic that had been used to brew the tincture than with any floral properties.

"How long has it been?" she asked, not expecting an

answer. "I imagine you're lonely. But you'd do better with a real healer."

The glass and the vial were whisked away, and she got the impression she'd hurt the helper's feelings. She sighed in defeat. "Maybe I'll stay a few days, long enough to get things in order here and recover my strength. I know I can't get on the road again yet. I wouldn't make it very far now. But if I'm going to stay any longer, we'll need provisions. I imagine you've used up what was left in the house. But I'll need money for that, or something to trade, and you'll need to let me out of the house."

The jar of elder flowers rose, then returned to the table with a thud. "Herbs? You think anyone would actually trade for them? They could have taken whatever they wanted from the garden." Then again, if the local healer had been anything like Mother Alis, no one would have dared set foot in her garden, even after she was gone. Healers were respected, but they were also feared, and a garden like this would contain a variety of plants mixed together. Someone would have to know what they were doing to be sure to harvest the right thing rather than something potentially dangerous.

She finished her meal and the tea, then put on her boots and went out to the shed. There was thyme, rosemary, dill, mint, and lavender hanging from the ceiling, with some flowers remaining on the lavender. Those were herbs people could use. It was early for this year's growth to be ready for harvest, so unless they'd grown and dried herbs for themselves, they might need a supply. She made up a few smaller bundles, tying them off with string she found in the shed, and put them in a basket. In the garden, she snipped some early chives and parsley, then she took her basket and headed toward the market square. Even if there wasn't a market in progress that morning, she could sit there and sell to passers-by, if there were any. If all else failed, she could try going door-to-door. The castle on the hill probably had its own kitchen garden, but as a very last resort she could try there and hope they'd take pity on her out of charity.

As she approached the village center, she saw that there were more people than she'd expected, though still not many. A few of the windows that had been shuttered the previous evening were open, and she saw people on the lane. In the square, several carts had been set up as stalls around the market pillar. A few people browsed the wares. It wasn't a lively scene, but she spotted cheese, vegetables, and sacks of what might be flour. As she approached, she eavesdropped on the banter among the vendors. The miller and the vegetable seller were teasing the dairy maid, but they were apparently outclassed in the battle of wits. Elwyn didn't catch what the dairy maid said, but both men laughed, and the miller said, "I'm surprised your sour tongue doesn't curdle your milk."

"Don't you know, curdling the milk is an important part of the cheesemaking process," the dairy maid said with a laugh. "My temperament is ideally suited to my trade, and you have to admit I make the finest cheese around."

"You make the only cheese around," the miller said.

The dairy maid turned and addressed Elwyn. "You look like a woman of refined taste. You try this and tell these louts that it's the finest cheese you've ever had." She sliced a bit of cheese off a wheel on her cart and held it out to Elwyn.

Elwyn had thought no one had noticed her, so she was taken aback at the realization she'd been seen. Of course she'd been seen, she chided herself. She hadn't become an invisible helper, and she'd come to the market to trade. She could hardly trade without being seen. She took the cheese and forced herself to eat it slowly and thoughtfully to assess the quality rather than devouring it eagerly. It had been so long since she'd had cheese at all, let alone good cheese, and this cheese was very good. "I like this," she said after she'd finished chewing and swallowing. "A good, complex flavor. It's been aged, hasn't it?"

The maid beamed. "I knew you had refined taste. You must hail from more civilized parts. I haven't seen you around here before. I'm Mair." She was probably close to Elwyn's age, in her mid-thirties. Her eyes were very blue in her tanned face, and her curly light-brown hair, streaked with sun, hung loose around her shoulders.

"I'm stopping by briefly," Elwyn said, avoiding giving her name. The less that could be used to track her, the better.

"Well, welcome. It's always good to have someone new to talk to." Mair turned back to her cart and scooped some white cheese out of a pot, scraped it onto a chunk of bread, and handed it to Elwyn. "Now, try this one. This is something new I've been experimenting with, a goat cheese. I only have a few goats now, but I may get more if people like the cheese."

Again, Elwyn had to resist the urge to wolf down the food. She took small bites, savoring each one. "It's good, but it's missing something. Have you considered adding herbs to it? I have some fresh chives that would liven it up." She held up her basket.

Mair picked up a bundle of chives from the basket, sniffed them, and said, "I remember my father used to make an herbed goat cheese. But then Mother Dilys left and we haven't had a proper herbalist."

Elwyn glanced around the tiny market and the nearly empty village. "It seems a lot of people left."

"Rydding isn't what it once was. Not that it was ever big. I'll trade you this cheese for these chives. Oh, and you have fresh parsley. That, too." She took the herbs she wanted from the basket, then handed over a chunk of cheese that Elwyn was sure was worth far beyond the value of the herbs. Her pride wanted her to refuse, but she couldn't afford to turn away any food.

"Done," she said, taking the cheese.

"Is that lavender?" Mair asked as she dug further in Elwyn's basket.

"I'm afraid it's rather old."

Mair lifted a bundle and sniffed it. "It still smells good, and my linens need refreshing. I'll take some of that, too. How about a bit of goat cheese for that?" She took the lavender and turned to her cart, where she scooped some of the soft cheese into a smaller crock. "You can return the crock when you're done," she said, handing it to Elwyn. "I'm at the market most days, or you can find me at the dairy by the bridge." Now Elwyn knew she was being given charity. Kindness, she told herself. It was kindness, and there was no shame in being the recipient of kindness.

"What happened here? It's a lovely village to be so empty."

Mair's friendly, open face closed. "People drifted away. Then there wasn't enough business for most of the rest, and they drifted away. And so forth."

Elwyn thanked her and made her way to the miller. It would probably be easier to buy bread, and the aroma coming from the nearby bakery was tempting, but flour would be less expensive, and she was sure the helper could make something of it. She held a bundle of dried mint out to the miller. "This will help keep the mice out of your stock."

He sniffed the bundle. "I used to get mint from Mother Dilys," he said.

"Be sure you give her a fair deal," Mair called out. "We want to keep her here. This village could use an herbalist."

The miller glanced at Mair before scooping some flour into a cloth bag. He said "I'll take all the mint you've got and trade you for this. And then we'll make arrangements for a regular delivery. The mice are eating me out of business."

"Mint's just starting to come up well, but I still have some dried stock, and I can make sachets for you."

He gave her a wolfish smile. "I'd be glad to stop by sometime and pick them up."

"I'm sure I'll see you around the market," she said. It didn't sound as though herbs were what he'd really be hoping to get if he visited.

She was trading more lavender for a cabbage when a voice called out, "You need some eggs." She turned to see a bundle of shawls with a chicken perched on top sitting on the steps at the foot of the market pillar. After studying the bundle more carefully, she saw that there was a wizened face peering out from under the top shawl. The bundle was an old woman with a chicken on her head, several more scratching the ground beside her, and a basket of eggs in front of her.

"I'm afraid I don't have any money," Elwyn said. "Do you need any herbs?"

The woman snorted. "Not likely. But I have more eggs than I can possibly use. The chickens have been busy. Take what you need. There may come a time when I need something from you, and I hope you'll return the kindness."

Elwyn wasn't sure if she was getting herself into a dangerous bargain or was merely being given charity, but eggs would make for a heartier meal than she'd had in a very long time. She knelt and took a few eggs. "Thank you."

"Mayhap I'll get a cough and need a tonic. I also collect table scraps to feed the chickens. Mostly, they forage in the woods and come home at night, but I like to give them treats and make bonemeal for them. But you probably use scraps for compost to grow your herbs."

"I haven't had any scraps yet," Elwyn said. "And I'm not sure how long I'll be staying."

"If the village brought you here, it's because you need to be here."

"It looks like the village could do with some people. It seems to be practically abandoned."

"Everyone's still here, except for the ones who left."

The woman had perhaps spent too much time in the company of her chickens, so Elwyn smiled, thanked her again, and headed home—to the cottage; it was dangerous to think of it as home—with her bounty. At least the people here seemed to appreciate the value of her knowledge. She should be able to survive long enough by trading the existing stock to get her feet back under her before she had to move on.

She deposited her purchases in the kitchen and said, "I'm perfectly capable of cooking for myself, but if you want to make something of this, that would also be lovely. I don't want to get in your way." There was work to be done in the garden, but the trip to the market had sapped her meager strength. A couple of good meals and a comfortable night's sleep hadn't made up for the months of privation. She should probably rest before trying to do anything else.

She woke from an unintentional nap in the armchair in

the sitting room later in the afternoon to find that she'd been covered with a light blanket. A steaming cup of tea and a small cake sat on the table beside her and a warm glow filled her at the simple caring that represented. She could get used to this kind of treatment, which meant she should probably move on before she got too spoiled.

CHAPTER 3

E lwyn woke the next morning in a dark room with rain spattering on the panes of the dormer windows. It looked like there would be no work in the garden for her until the rain passed. Since she had nowhere to go and nothing in particular to do, she let herself fall back to sleep. It was still gray and rainy when she woke again. She dressed and headed downstairs, where she found a griddle cake with honey drizzled over it and a cup of tea. The tea and cake were still hot, but she knew the helper had ways to keep food warm, since the work of healers didn't always fit around mealtimes. It felt rather indulgent to take advantage of that power for mere laziness.

After breakfast, she went to the bookshelf in the sitting room in search of something to amuse her, since she was stuck indoors. The books left behind included a few treatises on remedies, as well as one dog-eared novel with a battered leather cover. She had copies of the treatises in her personal library that she'd had to leave behind. It would be good to have those references handy again—that was, it would be good if she were planning to resume her work. As it was, she would leave them behind for the next person when she left. She didn't see the house's log, the record kept by the resident healers of patients and treatments. It should have remained with the house so the next occupant would know the medical histories of the people served by the local healer, so Mother Dilys was unlikely to have taken it with her. Elwyn reminded herself that she wasn't staying, and if the helper saw her reading the log, it might get ideas.

She picked up the novel and sat in the chair. She'd never had much time to read for pleasure, and this was the sort of novel that was purely for entertainment, with little literary merit. She wanted to sneer at it, but she soon got so caught up in the story that she jumped when she heard a knock. Had she only imagined it because someone had knocked on a door in the book, or had it come from somewhere in the cottage? No, that was definitely a knock, she decided when it happened again.

She set her book down and got up to go out into the hall. At the next knock, she could hear that the sound was coming from the back door. She edged back toward the sitting room, hoping that the visitor hadn't seen her through the lace curtains in the door's small window. Who could it be? Dire scenarios raced through her mind. Had the baron's men tracked her down already? Were the local authorities coming to evict her as a squatter? She could flee through the front door, unless they'd stationed someone there to block her escape, but she wanted to run upstairs to grab her belongings first. Could she do that before they rushed inside?

She was still standing frozen, unsure what to do, when the door opened to reveal an utterly drenched Mair standing on the doorstep. Elwyn lunged forward to make it look like she'd been the one to open the door. She'd have words with the helper later. "Ah, I was right!" Mair said. "I suspected you'd be in this cottage if you had herbs. Since it was too rainy for a market, I thought I'd experiment with seasoning the cheese," she said. "Would you like to help me test it?"

As much as Elwyn was inclined to keep to herself, she couldn't leave her neighbor out in the rain, especially not if she came bearing cheese. "Come inside," she urged, stepping back from the door. "There's a fire in the kitchen."

When they reached the kitchen, Mair took a seat at the table and opened the bundle she carried. It contained a small crock and a loaf of bread. She took the lid off the crock, revealing a cheese with bits of green mixed in. Elwyn looked for plates and a knife, realizing she didn't know where anything was kept. She noticed movement on one of the shelves and smiled a thanks to the helper as that drew her attention to the plates. The knife on the sideboard practically leaped into her hand. She set the plates on the table and handed Mair the knife.

Mair sliced bread, then spread cheese on the slices and handed one to Elwyn. Elwyn was still so unaccustomed to having food that anything would have tasted good, but this was delightful. "Excellent," she said when she finished chewing.

"I think so, too," Mair said with a nod. "I might even be able to take this to market in a larger town. There aren't many people to sell to around here."

"I didn't notice any shops in the village."

"There aren't any, not anymore. There aren't enough people to keep them open. That's why we do the daily market. It's easier for people than having to go out to the dairy, over to the greengrocer's farm, and out to the mill. Though the miller only comes to market once a week. You don't need to buy flour daily. The baker's the only one who keeps a shop, since it's right there on the square anyway, and she'll also bake your goods in her oven. There are peddlers who come through every so often for other goods, and when anyone goes to another town, they take orders from everyone else and bring their goods to sell. We take turns going."

"So, you can come and go from this place," Elwyn said with a smile, forcing herself not to look at the bread and cheese as though she wanted more. "I was beginning to worry that I'd stumbled into some sort of enchanted village separated from the real world." Actually, that would have been nice. It would have meant that the people who were pursuing her wouldn't be able to find her.

"Sometimes it does feel that way, but no. It's far too easy to leave. We're not on the way to anywhere else, so not too many people find us. How did you come across us?"

"I didn't want to be on the main road anymore, and I saw a byway that looked pleasant and shady. Then I came upon the village and the door to this cottage was open. No one seemed to have been here in a long time, so I thought I might as well pass the night."

"I'm glad you did. It seems like the people who need to be here find their way here. Everyone who's come in the past ten or so years has been someone who needed to find a place. We just need more of them to have a proper village once more."

Elwyn pondered that. Had there been something leading her here? It had almost felt like it. Or it had merely been the first lane she saw after she decided she didn't want to die on the side of the main road. She'd seen nothing to indicate there was an enchantment on this place.

26

"So, you're taking over the cottage?" Mair asked. "You seem to know your herbs."

Elwyn tensed, but Mair didn't sound like she was being critical, merely curious. "I stumbled upon it when I arrived the other night," Elwyn said. "I grew up in a house like this, helping the local herbalist, and it appeared to have been abandoned, though it's well-kept, so I thought I'd see if I could stay until I was ready to travel again."

"Oh, it's been abandoned, and if you grew up in a house like this, I'm sure you know why it's well-kept." Mair winked. "If you've been welcomed in, then maybe it's the right place for you. We could use someone who knows their herbs here. I'll need to place a standing order for parsley and chives for this cheese."

"I don't know if I can stay. Who would I approach about renting it?"

Mair smiled. "That's one good thing about what's happened here. There is no rent. If no one's living there, just stake your claim. That's what most of the people here do."

"What about . . ." Elwyn gestured with her head in the general direction of the castle looming over the village.

"No one's heard from the lord in years. He probably died without heirs and no one's bothered to claim the place. We get by just fine without him. Besides, I didn't think healers were ever expected to pay rent. The cottage comes with the job."

"I'm not really a healer," Elwyn protested. "I can't take on that job. And I can't stay here for long."

Mair coughed, and Elwyn said instinctively, "That doesn't sound good. You might have taken a chill. I'll make some tea. What sort of thing do you like?"

"Oh, I don't know. Whatever you think best."

It wasn't for healing, so the stakes were pretty low.

There was no real harm she could do here if she read wrong, and she wouldn't have to go deep to sense Mair's tastes. As she got up to go to the kettle, she brushed against Mair and opened her magical senses. Feelings flooded her—contentment, warmth, but also loneliness and loss. Mair wanted sweet, but also tart. Elwyn broke the connection and said, "I think I have just the thing." She mixed together the herbs that would create the flavor she thought would most appeal to Mair, adding in some elderflowers and dried elderberries to help fight off a cough or cold. That hardly counted as healing. It was merely about knowing her herbs.

"I thought people with your skills were in high demand," Mair remarked while Elwyn poured hot water into a teapot. "Not wandering the countryside and settling into abandoned cottages. Or is that how you find a new position? You wander until you find an empty healer's cottage that fate pointed you to?"

"It's not so much about not being able to find a position," Elwyn said, wincing.

"It was a man, wasn't it?" Mair said with a knowing nod. "It usually is. They ruin everything. What did this one do?"

"It's more what he didn't do. He didn't support me when another man accused me, and I couldn't stay there any longer."

"Of course. And I'm sure he's still secure in his position."

"As far as I know." Elwyn had to smile at the idea that a healer would ever oust a nobleman.

"Well, you'll have very little to worry about here, as there are no men to speak of, and they're all married. I suppose they can still be a problem, but not that kind of problem, unless they're being utter rats. And that does happen." She heaved a dramatic sigh. "No, I'm sorry, but men may still be a problem here, alas. Word of advice: Get your flour at the market, in public. Never be alone at the mill with the miller unless his wife is present. She's nice, if a bit of a wet hen, but he has wandering hands. If you absolutely must go, wear something dark so the handprints will show. His hands always have flour on them."

"I'll keep that in mind," Elwyn said dryly. "I already got that impression from him at the market."

"You are quite discerning. If this village is going to draw people who need it, and who we need, I'd like it to start bringing us some eligible men. Young—but not too young —useful, with plenty of skills. Handsome, of course. I could use a farmhand. An attractive one with broad shoulders who takes his shirt off to work on hot summer days." Her eyes took on a wistful look.

"You run the dairy on your own?"

"There's not that much work. The goats and cows graze on the meadow, I milk them, and while they graze, I make cheese and butter." She leaned forward. "I don't suppose you know anything about healing animals. Mother Dilys used to help me when the cows were giving birth."

"I know herbs," Elwyn said, turning away from the table to find the strainer the helper nudged toward her. She poured a cup of tea and pushed the cup across the table to Mair. "I have some honey if it's not sweet enough."

Mair sniffed the drink, then took a sip. "No, this is lovely. It tastes like summer. Almost like it has honey in it."

Elwyn poured herself a cup and resumed her seat at the table. They sat in quiet companionship, sipping their tea while the rain poured outside. Elwyn couldn't remember the last time she'd had a kitchen-table chat with another woman. Certainly not in her last position or the one before that. A neighbor might have stopped by occasionally in her previous position. Otherwise, it had been in the time she'd spent with Mother Alis, both when she hid out there during her childhood and later when she went to train with her. That cottage always had women gathered around the kitchen table.

"This is nice," Mair said after another sip of tea. "It's been a long time since I just sat at a table with a friend, chatting. It's been somewhat lonely here since everyone left, and the rest of us don't meet up nearly as often as we should. Ever since the inn closed, there's nowhere to go other than each other's kitchens." She emptied her cup and said, "This was wonderful, but I need to get back to the dairy. There's butter to be churned. Thank you for the tea and the conversation."

Elwyn walked her to the door. "The rain seems to be letting up," she said when she opened it.

"You are quite the optimist. It's as dreary as ever." Mair pulled her shawl up over her head and said, "I enjoyed our chat. You should stop by the dairy. But be warned, I'll make you try cheese until you never want to see it again."

Elwyn found that hard to believe. She was still smiling when she closed the door. "I think I know what to do to earn money," she said out loud. "The front room would make a nice tea shop. I can use my knowledge of herbs without actually doing any healing."

She didn't know if the helper would be agreeable with that, but when she woke from an afternoon nap (there wasn't much else she could do on a rainy day, and her body did need to recover), the front room had been turned into a proper tea shop. Small tables and chairs from the spare room upstairs had been set up in front of the windows, each covered with a cloth and topped with a doily. Teacups, teapots, and jars of herbs filled the shelves. "I take it that means you're fine with this plan," she said.

Elwyn figured the best way to spread the news was to tell Mair, so the next morning she found her at the market and said, "After what you said about needing a place to gather, I decided I'd open a tea shop in my front room. People can come to drink tea and chat, and if they like the tea, they can buy some to take home. I'll open it in the afternoons, when people might have a spare moment after chores."

"Excellent idea. I'll be sure everyone knows."

Mair was the first to arrive that afternoon, with a pretty young woman of about thirty. "This is Lucina, the baker," she said, then frowned at Elwyn. "You know, I don't think I caught your name."

"Oh, did I not introduce myself?" Elwyn said. If others knew her name, that would increase the chances of word getting out about where she was. Her name wasn't rare, but she didn't know how many herbalists and healers named Elwyn there were. But she hated to lie to someone who'd become her closest friend. "I'm Wyn," she said. It had been a childhood nickname, but she hoped that it wasn't so similar to her real name that it would be immediately connected to her. "And forgive my terrible manners in not introducing myself earlier."

"We just started talking as though we've known each other forever, and it seems to have slipped my mind that we weren't properly introduced." To Lucina Mair added, "Wyn has a knack for choosing just the right tea."

"Please, have a seat," Elwyn said, allowing herself to lightly touch both women as she escorted them to a table. From Mair she got the sense of tension and tiredness. Lucina's emotions were more volatile, a mix of sadness and rage, all covered in overwhelming exhaustion. Both of them could use something calming, she decided.

"You got this set up quickly," Mair remarked as Elwyn prepared a blend of herbs for the tea. To Lucina she explained, "This room was completely empty yesterday."

"All of these things were already in the house," Elwyn said. "Did Mother Dilys run a tea shop?"

"Not exactly, but she liked to do her consultations over a cup of tea at one of these tables, so it was something similar."

Elwyn watched as both women visibly relaxed once they began drinking the tea. "I should have brought my cakes and buns that didn't sell this morning," Lucina said. "People might want to have something to eat with their tea. I'll bring some by tomorrow, and we can split the proceeds."

"Well, first I'll need customers," Elwyn said.

"They'll come," Mair assured her. "Word will spread. It just takes people time to warm up to new ideas."

However, Mair and Lucina were the only customers that afternoon, until just before Elwyn was planning to close the shop, when a stocky woman stood in the doorway, glaring at her. "How dare you usurp this cottage for something as trivial as a tea shop," she said.

CHAPTER 4

"Excuse me?" Elwyn asked the woman. "This is a cottage for a healer. You can't just open a tea shop here."

That stung, since the woman wasn't entirely wrong, but Elwyn didn't want to admit that to her. Forcing herself to remain calm, she said stiffly, "The teas are made from herbs and provide health benefits. I have one that I think would help you considerably if you'd like to come in and have a seat."

The woman didn't budge. "Not just anyone can move in here and set up shop."

"I assure you, I've been properly trained. I have extensive expertise in herbs."

"But are you a real healer? I know about these things, and you can't just move in to one of these cottages. You have to be a proper healer, and you have to be chosen."

Although Elwyn had been denying all along that she planned to work as a healer, this woman made her want to declare herself the new town healer, just to spite her. Instead, she forced a polite smile and said, "If you know about these things, you would know that I wouldn't last long in this cottage if I wasn't welcome. I am seeing to things here for the time being as a guest of this cottage. Now, would you like some tea?"

"I'll be keeping an eye on you," the woman said with a huff, then spun around stalked off.

Elwyn felt somewhat vindicated in her assertion that she was welcome when the door slammed shut behind the woman without Elwyn touching it. "Thank you," she said to the helper. In spite of what she'd said to the woman, she did feel a bit guilty about not using the cottage for its intended purpose. The resident helper was supposed to make life easier for the healer, as it was difficult to care for oneself and care for the community. If the healer didn't have to cook, clean, and do laundry for herself, she was better able to help her patients. It felt a bit like cheating to get all that help when she was merely running a tea shop without seeing patients, but she was quite ill-equipped to look after herself. She'd had servants in her father's home, so she'd never cooked a meal or washed her own laundry until she went to work for Mother Alis. Mother Alis had made her learn the basics so she'd better understand what her patients experienced and so she could do what was needed if she visited a bedridden patient, but she hadn't done that sort of work in all her years at court.

The next day, the shop was busier. Most of the women in the village were unmarried, and they seemed to enjoy having a place to go to socialize away from their homes. Elwyn could see what Mair had meant about the town needing to attract more men.

"It looks like it's going well," Mair said when she arrived with another woman she introduced as Nesta, the miller's wife.

"Yes. I was worried there might be some resistance, though."

"Oh, you must have had a visit from Sara Smith," Mair said. "Stocky woman with a glare that could curl iron?"

Elwyn fought the urge to shudder. "Yes."

"Don't worry about her, even if she doesn't need a forge, anvil, and hammer to bend metal. She wants things to go back to the way they were before, and that makes her hate all newcomers she sees as getting in the way of that. If you're in the cottage, Mother Dilys can't come back. Not that she would. She said there was too much for her to do while retired, not enough to keep her busy while working, and she left. She was reunited with her first love, after all those years, if you can believe it. She always was a hopeless romantic. Sara doesn't represent the views of the village. After all, the Chicken Lady likes you."

"Well, if the Chicken Lady likes me, I should be set," Elwyn said with a smile.

"Nesta needs a moment to relax," Mair said. She added to the other woman, "Elwyn knows how to pick just the right tea. Somehow, she can tell exactly what you want, even if you don't know, yourself." Elwyn thought that was overstating things, but she didn't want to let her friend down, so she let her hand brush against Nesta's and read the need for sweet and calm.

"I have something you might like," she said, then went behind the counter and made a blend of herbs and set it to steep.

"It's nice to get away from the house for a moment," Nesta said, wringing her hands on top of the table.

"Now, what's upsetting you so much?" Mair asked. To Elwyn, she added, "When she got to my house, she was in such a state that I knew I had to bring her here. You'd have just the thing."

"I'm worried about my husband," Nesta blurted, and her shoulders shook.

"Oh no, what is it?" Elwyn asked. "What are his symptoms?"

"Not that! No!" Nesta leaned forward and said softly to Mair, "I think he may be straying."

Mair laughed, leaning her head back as she roared, then she wiped tears from the corners of her eyes and patted Nesta's hand. "I can assure you he isn't. Not for lack of trying, I'm afraid, but none of us will have him, so you're quite safe."

Nesta sat utterly frozen for a moment before she, too, laughed. "I don't know whether to be relieved or insulted on his behalf," she finally said.

"I'm not sure he really means it. He probably wouldn't know what to do if one of us took him up on a proposition. I suggest you try flirting with him the way he does with the village women and see what he does." She winked. "Could be fun."

Elwyn was glad that neither of them were looking at her because she couldn't keep a straight face.

"I suppose I worry because there are all these women in the village, and so few men. I felt like he could have his pick of women."

"I know I'm not interested in him," Mair said, "so you have nothing to fear from me. Lucina seems to have gone off men, as well." She turned toward Elwyn. "What about you? It sounded like you've gone off men, too."

"For the time being," Elwyn said mildly as she poured tea. "Things didn't end well with the last one."

"So, see, you have nothing to worry about," Mair said to Nesta. "Don't you feel better?"

Nesta finally laughed. More of her tension drained away after she drank the tea, and by the time she left, she had lost the anxious look she'd had when she arrived.

Mair lingered after the others had left. "You're doing a lot of good with this, you know," she said to Elwyn. "Did you notice young Hana?"

Elwyn tried to remember all the women who'd been in the shop that afternoon. "The quiet one?"

"Yes. This is the first time I've managed to coax her out of her house. She's a weaver and she claims she needs to work, but I think it's more that she's afraid of others. She found her way to us during the winter. I get the impression that she was fleeing something, perhaps a bad employer. Having somewhere safe to go made a big difference for her."

"That's good to hear." It appeared Elwyn wasn't the only fugitive in the village. Again, she had to wonder if it was merely a place situated where people trying to stay off the main roads would find it or if there was something else about it that drew people in need of safety. That was a pretty fantasy, but she feared she couldn't count on being entirely safe from the outside world. She'd probably have to move on eventually, but every coin she made in the shop improved her chances of surviving when she had to flee.

One afternoon before Elwyn opened the shop, Lucina came by with that day's buns and cakes. Instead of just dropping them off and taking her share of the previous day's sales, she paused, taking a few deep breaths, as though working up the courage to make a request. "I need your help," she blurted.

"Yes, of course," Elwyn said. "What do you need?"

Lucina closed her eyes, as though in deep pain. "I need to sleep," she said, her voice heavy with weariness. "Your teas make me feel better, and I wonder if there's anything else you can do for me."

Lucina truly appeared to be in distress, and even though she no longer considered herself a healer, Elwyn had sworn an oath to help those in need, and Lucina was a friend, so she couldn't turn her away. Besides, this wouldn't truly require her to use the gift she couldn't trust. It was merely an extension of what she did with teas.

"Let's have a seat," she said, guiding Lucina to one of the tables. "What kind of trouble are you having with sleep? Do you have difficulty falling asleep, or do you wake during the night? Is it because your mind is restless, or is it your body?"

Not meeting Elwyn's eyes, Lucina stared down at the table and whispered, "I want to sleep without nightmares. Can you give me something that will give me deep, restful sleep without dreams?"

"Dreams are a part of restful sleep. You can't block them entirely for long without suffering ill effects."

Lucina's shoulders sagged. "Oh. So you can't help."

"I can't take the nightmares away for good. But sometimes just a few days of the body getting good rest can help the mind heal. You still need to address the source of your nightmares to have a long-term cure."

"How would I do that?" The baker's voice was rough with emotion.

"Talk about it with someone you trust."

"I can't do that," Lucina said, shaking her head violently.

"Then talk to thin air. Just saying it aloud may help. Or write it down. That may help you look at your worries objectively. I assume that your nightmares are based on something real. It's not a monster under the bed or walking through the village naked."

The slightest hint of a smile crossed Lucina's face, lighting her countenance for a moment. Then the shadows returned. "Yes. They're real. I keep reliving the worst day of my life."

Based on her name, her darker coloring, and her accent, Elwyn guessed that she was from Tufana, where there had been a great deal of unrest in the past decade. A refugee who'd escaped the violence would have plenty of fuel for nightmares. She seemed to be yet another person who'd found refuge in Rydding.

Elwyn stood and went behind the counter to her shelves of herbs. "I can give you something that will help you rest and that will take away some of your anxiety," she said. "A few good nights of sleep may help give you the strength to face your fears so you can do better in the long term. First, a brew that may help you now while I prepare the blend that you'll drink an hour before you go to bed." She mixed the right herbs and spooned them into a small teapot, then poured hot water over them. "This may make you a bit drowsy, but it should relax you. It's even stronger than some of the calming teas I've made for you before."

How had she missed the depth of Lucina's distress? She was clearly exhausted all the time and had dark hollows under her eyes, but Elwyn had assumed it was merely due to her schedule, which required her to be up hours before dawn. If she'd been thinking like a healer, she would have noticed it had to be more than that. It seemed that even when she wasn't trying to be a healer, she still failed at it.

"I've already done the day's baking," Lucina said. "I

start very early, so I'm ready for a nap by this time. I would be delighted to fall asleep soon."

While waiting for the tea to brew, Elwyn mixed a blend of herbs in a clean jar. She wrapped a ribbon around it. In a second jar, she put one of the herbs without the others. She strained the tea into a cup and added a few drops from small vials and a spoonful of honey. This blend should help Lucina relax and put the past behind her. She brought the cup to Lucina and said, "Drink this now. Then an hour before bedtime, make a cup of tea using one spoon of this blend with a cup of boiling water and steep for five minutes." She indicated the jar with a ribbon around it. "When you've used that up, continue making a nightly brew with this other jar. You'll have a few nights of deep sleep. Over time, you may rest more regularly."

Lucina took a sip of the brew and sighed. "I feel better already."

With a smile, Elwyn said, "The scent is relaxing on its own, but it can't have done much for you yet."

"Having hope helps a great deal, as does knowing someone cares." That sent another stab of guilt through Elwyn for not having noticed a friend's suffering.

"Well, you just sit and relax and drink that. Breathe the scent and take deep breaths." Elwyn had to admit that it felt good to be back at her old trade. There was something about knowing exactly the right combination of herbs and essences that would address a particular problem that was not only satisfying, but actually a little thrilling. She'd missed it. But she also feared it. What if she failed again? Worse, what if word got out that there was a healer, and that word spread beyond the village? Someone might recognize her description and she'd be caught.

She didn't know if Lucina had told others, but several

other customers began asking for teas particular to certain ailments. She offered teas to treat coughs, congestion, and digestive upsets, and her insomnia treatments were popular. Then the greengrocer showed her a rash on his hands. That required a salve rather than a tea, so she moved beyond merely selling tea. Still, this work wasn't too far removed from what she did when finding just the right tea for a person, so she didn't consider herself to be acting as a healer, and she didn't use her magical gift for recommending treatments, just her expertise and training. None of the ailments she treated were life-or-death, so she couldn't do much harm if she failed.

Some of Elwyn's customers bartered with whatever goods they produced, but several paid in coin.That meant that when the peddler came to the market, Elwyn had money to spend. She was able to restock on real tea, as well as a few spices, though she was careful not to buy enough that it would be obvious an herbalist was in business, in case the peddler had seen any wanted posters, and she bought cloth to make some new clothes that weren't as worn as what she'd had on the road. The helper turned out to be as skilled with a needle as it was in the kitchen because she woke the next morning with a new dress hanging on the hook in her room. It had more flounces on it than she would have liked, but it was nice having fresh clothing.

Everything was going so well that she was starting to worry that something was sure to go wrong. This was when the baron's men would find her and drag her away, after one of her new friends betrayed her. Or her friends would find out what had happened and run her out of town. It was too good to last. She started to think she should plan her departure and leave before her past caught up with her.

She had new clothing and money, and she'd stayed longer in this place than she had at any other place since she'd fled the duke's court. It was time to move on, but she kept delaying, telling herself she'd stay one more day. All the while, she couldn't escape the sense that something was bound to happen.

It turned out she was right, though not in any way she'd expected.

One morning, she went out to the garden to pick some berries for breakfast. She saw a glint of metal from near the berry vines and went over to see what it was. She fought back a yelp when she saw a man lying there.

"I knew I should have left yesterday," she muttered.

CHAPTER 5

The man wore armor on his upper body and had a sword on his belt. Elwyn didn't see any insignia on his armor, but an armored man in her garden was a bad sign. Had the baron found her? Was this one of his men? She wasn't even sure he was alive. If he was dead, would she be accused of his murder? She wanted to rush inside, pack her belongings and as much food as she could, and flee. On the other hand, although she had abandoned her calling, she had sworn an oath to provide aid where it was needed. There was no other healer nearby. If she abandoned him, then she truly would have failed as a healer, regardless of what had happened in the past.

She knelt beside him and picked up his hand, placing her fingers against his wrist. He had a pulse, a little weaker and more rapid than it should have been, but he was alive. She clasped his hand in hers and opened her senses, going deeper than she'd allowed herself to go when reading her friends to select tea for them. She immediately felt a sharp pain in her upper side, just under her armpit, and an ache on the side of her cheek. A more detailed scan showed that

43

the cheek was merely bruised. The wound on the side had slashed across his ribs but had hit nothing vital. She felt the clammy, shaky sense of shock, probably from loss of blood. She didn't find any injury in his head, so the unconsciousness must have been either from pain or shock, or possibly both of them in combination with exhaustion.

She doubted he'd been wounded in her garden. Surely she or the helper would have heard something if a fight had happened just outside, and the plants around him weren't disturbed. He must have reached the cottage and collapsed after being wounded elsewhere.

At the moment, though, it didn't matter who he was or why he'd come. She was obligated to treat him. Unfortunately, the helper couldn't leave the house to help her bring him inside, and it wouldn't be able to lift the man. If it was like the one she'd known growing up, the magic that created it kept it from being able to directly affect humans. Otherwise, the one in this cottage would probably carry her to bed when she stayed up late and force any potential couples into each other's arms.

Dragging him wouldn't be good for his wound, but he didn't have any injuries that would be complicated by moving him, so she got the wheelbarrow out of the shed. She rolled him into it and adjusted him so that his head rested at the top and his legs dangled over the end. Trying to move as smoothly as possible, she wheeled him to the back door. It was a good thing this part of the garden wasn't visible from the road and no one could see past the trees on either side of the garden. Otherwise, the neighbors were sure to wonder about her hauling a man to her house in a wheelbarrow. Then again, her closest neighbor was Mair, and she'd find it amusing and intriguing. She'd want to know if the man was handsome.

Elwyn looked down at his face. She supposed he might be considered handsome, though it was hard to tell while he was unconscious and sprawled over the wheelbarrow. He had brown hair that fell across his forehead and a long, straight nose. He certainly wasn't ugly, but she'd always felt that it was what was inside that made someone attractive, and that didn't show now.

The helper opened the door for her, and she eased the man out of the wheelbarrow onto the floor of the hall at the foot of the stairs. "I'll need medical supplies," she said. "Bandages, hot water, witch hazel, silk and a needle for sutures, and the comfrey cream. Or arnica, whichever we have. Is there any tincture of calendula? And a blanket." While the helper rounded up the supplies, she gingerly removed the wounded man's sword belt and armor. She'd done that far too often at tournaments while she was employed at the duke's court and sometimes in the duke's chambers after the tournament. The duke had liked to set an example by going full-tilt, even against younger knights, then expected her to set things to rights afterward, away from the eyes of the court.

The last time she'd removed a man's armor, though, it hadn't been the duke's. It had been another wounded knight, and that was when she'd failed as a healer. She'd spent so much time dealing with the consequences of that particular knight's actions among the serving girls that she hadn't been as careful as she should have been. She must have missed something because he died in spite of her treatment, even though she hadn't thought his wounds were that severe. Since she hadn't been allowed to examine his body, she'd never know what she'd missed, and she couldn't even console herself with the thought that it had been unintentional. She hadn't wanted him to die, but she hadn't been all that worried about whether he would live.

Shaking herself out of the memory, she set the armor aside and saw that she'd been right about the wound, a slash between the breastplate and pauldron. He should have had a padded arming doublet, if not mail, beneath the armor to protect against wounds like this. All he had under the armor was a shirt that was soaked in blood. She peeled the fabric away from his skin and pushed it up to reveal the wound. His ribs had deflected the blow so that the wound didn't go deep enough to hit anything vital, but he wouldn't be raising his right arm or moving his torso much anytime soon. Whoever had attacked him had either known exactly where to strike him where he wasn't protected or had been very lucky.

A bowl of warm water and a cloth settled on the floor beside her. She soaked the cloth in the water and sponged the blood away from the wound so she could get a better look. What she saw matched what she'd read. She placed her hand gently on the wound itself and extended her senses once more. She didn't detect anything amiss. He'd be sore, but he should live.

She cut his shirt off so it wouldn't get in the way, poured water over the wound to wash it more thoroughly, then poured a witch hazel solution to clean the wound and slow the bleeding. He didn't so much as stir, though that should have stung. The wound was still bleeding, but slowly. It would need to be closed. She poured witch hazel over the needle and thread, then closed the wound with a row of stitches. The helper stood by with scissors to snip off the thread. A little blood oozed between the stitches, and she dabbed it away with more witch hazel. A vial of calendula tincture landed in her hand, and she dripped a few drops over the wound before she pressed her hand against it and sent healing energy into it. She then placed a pad of folded linen along the wound and secured it in place with a long bandage wrapped across his body and shoulder.

As she worked, she noted that he was lean and not particularly muscular. In her experience, knights were well-muscled from all the training with weapons. A man had to be strong to fight in armor and swing a sword, often for hours at a time. He looked to be about her age, so he was beyond being a page or squire. A knight that age should have had more muscles, and probably a few scars.

The armor was wrong, as well. Of course, he wouldn't have been riding around the countryside dressed in full tournament armor, but this armor was hardly functional, as though he'd dressed to look like a knight or soldier rather than to truly protect himself from attack. It was ill-fitting, incomplete, and put on badly. Which explained how he'd been wounded in spite of the armor. The gaps between pieces had been too big.

The more serious wound dealt with, she checked the bruise on his cheek. He'd taken a blow to the face, but recently, as the bruise was only just beginning to form. The spot was mostly red, but was starting to show bits of blue. She dabbed his cheek with arnica oil to speed healing. That done, she checked him over from head to foot, looking for any blood she hadn't noticed before. His limbs were whole, and she saw no sign of broken ribs. There was some mild bruising in places, but nothing that would cause much pain or impairment. It didn't appear that her empathic scan had missed anything, unless it was hidden deep within and causing no pain.

She pulled a blanket over him and sat back on her heels, studying her patient. The hallway floor couldn't be very comfortable, but he wouldn't be feeling that now. He needed to be warm, though. She knew she couldn't get him up the stairs to a bed, but she might be able to get him to the sitting room. "Can you please bring me the rug from in front of the sitting room fire?" she said to the helper. When the rug didn't come, she said, "He's not bleeding anymore, so he won't ruin it. You can bring a towel to put under him, and I'm sure you have the skill to get out any blood stains. Your rug won't be damaged."

Soon, the rug came slithering down the hall, as though it was crawling on its own. A towel landed on top of it. After thanking the helper, she lifted one side of the man and let the helper shove the rug under him. She then edged him over until he was lying on the rug, the towel under his wounded side, and she dragged the rug down the hall to the sitting room and then over to the fire, which flared up as the helper stoked it.

Just then, the bell she'd rigged so that she could hear from the living quarters when someone was at the door rang. That meant she likely had someone else in need of aid. A friendly visitor would have gone around to the back door. "I'd better go deal with that," she said. "Keep an eye on him and let me know discreetly if something seems to be wrong. I suspect he'll sleep right through it, but you never know."

She rinsed her hands and dried them, checking for any signs of blood on her knuckles or under her nails, before she stood and headed to the front door, where she found the miller, half crumpled in agony.

Remembering Mair's warning, she hurried to put the counter between herself and him after she let him inside. "What seems to be the trouble?" she asked, forcing a friendly smile.

"Well, you see, I get this grumbling in my gut . . ." he began, then launched into a list of symptoms so personal and, quite frankly, disgusting that she had to believe he really was in distress and wasn't merely using this as an excuse to be alone with her. He'd have to be delusional to think that a woman who'd heard such details about his bowels would have amorous feelings about him anytime soon. Just when she thought he'd listed everything that could possibly happen to a person's digestive system, he told her about even more symptoms. She fought the urge to glance over her shoulder as she wondered how her other patient was doing.

Finally, she had to ask, "What have you eaten? It sounds like your body is trying to purge something."

"I can't think of anything," he said with a shrug, not meeting her eyes. "Not unless Nesta is trying to poison me."

Elwyn was afraid she couldn't entirely rule that out, given what Nesta had recently learned about her husband. "And what about Nesta? Is she ill, as well?"

"Not that I've noticed."

If it was poison, his body was doing a good job of purging it. The best she could do was treat the symptoms. She packaged the recommended preparations, gave him instructions, and quoted the price. The miller must have been feeling bad because he didn't try to bargain. He didn't even try to flirt. He merely paid, took his purchases, and left, leaning forward slightly, as though guarding his belly.

She shut the door behind him, gave herself a dose of a preventative in case the miller had a communicable illness, and hurried back to the sitting room. Her patient still hadn't moved. His breathing was regular, and his pulse felt somewhat stronger. She even thought his color looked a bit better, though she wasn't sure if his pallor was because of his injury or if he was a fair-skinned person who seldom saw the sun. That was another oddity. Most of the knights she knew were suntanned. They wore their helmets for tournaments or battle, but they trained outdoors without them. Even those with fair skin had brown faces. He wore the armor of a knight, but not properly. He didn't have the muscles or the skin of a knight. When he woke, she'd have questions for him.

He could have been a prisoner, a knight who'd been confined for a long time. That would explain the pallor and lack of muscle tone, and he might not have had time to fully dress before escaping. The armor and sword would be most important, since they were hardest to replace. Her gaze turned in the direction of the castle, the top of the tallest tower barely visible above the trees through the window. What if it wasn't deserted? Were prisoners being held there? She shook her head to clear the flight of fancy. She was so eager to learn the mystery of what had happened in this village that she was imagining stories.

By this time, it was lunchtime, and she ate what the helper had prepared for her before checking on her patient once more. He was still unconscious, and he didn't react to her presence. She checked his wound, added more calendula tincture, put on a clean bandage and secured it once more, and all the while he didn't moan or stir, though she was sure that no matter how gentle she tried to be, she was causing him some pain. Now she was starting to worry. Maybe she'd missed something. This kind of profound unconsciousness usually indicated a serious head injury.

She pressed her hand against his head and opened her senses as wide as they would go. She felt nothing in his head other than the ache in his cheek, and that went no deeper. She could find nothing abnormal in his brain that would lead to remaining this insensate. Since she'd missed critical signs before, she inspected his head with her fingers, probing for lumps or dents. There was nothing. As far as she could tell, he was merely deeply asleep.

If he'd regained consciousness, she would have encouraged him to go back to sleep, possibly even given him a sleeping tonic, so she supposed there was no harm in letting him remain like this. That would help his body heal, and he was less likely to do something like tear a stitch that would cause him to lose more blood if he was asleep. This was far better than him being awake and insisting he was fine and didn't need to rest at all. She'd had far too many patients like that. Still, it was odd. She didn't think she'd ever had a patient with this kind of wound remain unconscious for this long.

It was soon time to open the tea shop. She would have preferred not to, but if she didn't open, she'd have to explain herself. She washed her hands, changed into a clean dress, and opened the shop. For once, she hoped she didn't have any customers. Money would be nice, especially if she had to flee again, but she was far too distracted to enjoy the company and she didn't want to have to answer questions about what was distracting her.

Mair arrived soon after the shop opened. "I need something soothing," she said, collapsing into a seat at one of the tables. "I've spent most of the day looking for a calf who strayed from his mother, who was so distraught that I couldn't milk her. I found the little bugger caught in a hedge near the brook, crying piteously, and yet he still fought me when I tried to free him. I would have been tempted to leave him there if his mother wasn't usually one of my best milkers. I'll be selling him off at the end of the summer, anyway."

While she talked, Elwyn brewed a pot of chamomile and lemon balm tea. "You don't keep the calves?"

"Not the males. I only need a bull to sire calves, and I need the calves so the cows produce milk. I keep the heifers and sell off the young bulls before they start challenging each other."

"What becomes of them?"

"I try not to think about it," Mair said wryly. "I like to think they're off siring their own herds, but I imagine they more likely end up on someone's plate or in someone's stew pot. But I can't afford to keep on anyone who doesn't make milk." With exaggerated brightness, she said, "So, how has your day gone?"

"Oh, the usual," Elwyn said, bringing over the teapot and two cups. She sat across from her friend and poured tea for both of them. She needed the relaxing brew as badly as Mair did. "Did you hear anything last night?"

Mair frowned in thought. "Not that I can think of, but I sleep like the dead. You could probably blow a trumpet outside my window in the middle of the night and I wouldn't stir. Why?"

"Oh, I thought I might have heard something, but I'm not sure whether or not I dreamed it."

"Pity. A little excitement might have been fun."

"Aside from a lost calf?"

"I'm not sure I'd call that exciting. At least not in an interesting way. You know what we need around here? A proper festival."

"With twenty people?"

"There are a few more than that. If it brings us all together with good food, maybe some music, it could be festive. We should plan something for midsummer. Who knows, maybe by then we'll have gained a few more people. I hope one of them's a musician. We don't have one here now, that I know of. You don't play an instrument, do you?"

"My mother made me learn the harp, long ago, but it's been years since I played."

"I can blow a few notes on a tin whistle. My father had a viol, but I haven't the slightest idea how to play it. This is why this village is so boring. No one here knows how to do anything other than their work. We don't know how to have fun. We had good festivals when I was a girl." She frowned as she took a sip of tea. "Though that may just be the golden glow of memory, and I'd find those festivals to be deadly dull now. I do remember wearing flowers in my hair and getting to stay up late. I remember there was dancing." She sighed. "I'm sure there was even a time when I danced with someone. Or perhaps I dreamed it. Do you dance?"

"I learned when I was young, but I'm afraid I've quite forgotten how. They probably don't do the same dances here."

"We don't do any dances here, so you could teach us what you remember. But for proper dancing, we need more men and, alas, those don't just fall out of the sky and land in our gardens."

Elwyn choked on the sip of tea she'd just taken. For a moment, she feared Mair had seen something. But if she had, she wouldn't have held back from talking about it. Little did her friend know that a man had, in fact, fallen into her garden. The question was, what kind of man was he?

Once she'd finished her tea, Mair said, "I brought you some butter, freshly churned. And now I have to get back home to see if my wayward calf has strayed yet again. That one's going to be trouble, I can tell. All men are, bovine or human."

After Mair's departure, Elwyn checked on the wounded man. He still showed no sign of waking. As much as she tried to reassure herself that he didn't have any kind of injury that would lead to profound unconsciousness, she still worried.

The one thing that might leave someone insensate for this long, aside from an injury, was magic. Elwyn's own powers were very limited. She could feel others' feelings and she could provide some healing energy, but she couldn't perform spells. She might be able to detect magic, though, if she looked for it.

This time, when she scanned her patient with her magical senses, she looked for signs of enchantment. She did pick up on some magical energy. She couldn't tell if this man was under a spell, but magic had been used on or around him recently. There was no way to undo a spell without the proper counterspell and the right abilities and training, but she did have some preparations that might help break him out of a magical trance.

Those weren't among the ones left behind by Mother Dilys. They were the few things she still had with her from her old life. She went up to her bedroom and dug in the bag she'd brought. At a noble court, enchantment was a constant threat, as many great lords kept court wizards to use against their enemies. Duke Maxen hadn't kept a wizard, but she had visited a friendly wizard to get some remedies against enchantment, and she'd been afraid that if she left them behind she'd have had witchcraft added to the accusations against her. Magic itself wasn't forbidden, but using it for harm was, and the mere presence of magical items could have been used as evidence to condemn her.

She should have left them somewhere once she fled so they couldn't be found on her if she was caught, but she hadn't been able to bear discarding something so precious that would be nearly impossible to replace. The vial she took from her bag wouldn't break a sleeping curse, but it would lessen the impact of any other magic that might be affecting him. She brought it downstairs, opened it, and knelt beside him to wave the open vial under his nostrils.

After a few moments, his eyelids fluttered. Then they opened, revealing bright blue eyes. "What happened? Where am I?" he mumbled. He frowned and added, "Who am I?"

CHAPTER 6

"I was rather hoping you could tell me that," Elwyn said. He blinked at her, looking dazed. "And who are you?"

"I'm the person who found you in my garden with a wound in your side and a bruise on your face. You must have been in a fight, though I can't tell if you were the winner or the loser."

"I don't feel like a winner," he said with a grimace.

"You're alive, with relatively minor wounds."

"What does the other guy look like?"

"I have no idea. He must have staggered to someone else's garden, if he didn't flee entirely."

"He's not here?"

"I can't see any sign of a fight having taken place here, and there was no other man in my garden. My nearest neighbor definitely would have let me know if she'd found a man—unless she wanted to keep him to herself."

"I had to have been hurt fairly badly for me to lose my memory," he said. He rubbed his head, then touched his bruised cheek and winced. "This must have been a blow."

"It's only a bruise. You don't have any head injuries."

"And how would you know that?"

"You were fortunate enough to collapse in the garden of a healer. Someone who knows something of healing," she hurried to correct herself.

"That was clever of me. I wonder if I did it on purpose. Thank you for coming to my aid. I'm afraid I can't introduce myself, but may I ask who you are?"

"I'm Wyn," she said, giving the same name she'd given to Mair. "And you're fortunate that I happened to be here. This cottage had been abandoned for years before I moved in not too long ago. And now, if you'll excuse me for a moment, I'll bring you something to help ease your aches."

"I would definitely appreciate that," he said heartily, closing his eyes.

She rose and went to the kitchen, where the helper was already brewing willow bark tea. "Just what I was coming to get," Elwyn said. "I think there's some kind of magic at work. My potion for diminishing the effects of magic was what woke him, and he has no memory, in spite of having no head injuries. There's something very odd about this whole situation." She reassured herself with the reminder that the duke hadn't kept a court wizard, so this likely had nothing to do with her own situation. It was merely a coincidence. This cottage was on the edge of the village, so obviously someone stumbling into the village who was growing weaker from his injury would go there first in search of aid. At least, that was what she told herself.

She took the tea to the sitting room and helped the man sit up so he could drink it. "Any dizziness?" she asked him. "Headache?"

"I feel somewhat lightheaded. And hungry. I don't know when I ate last—literally. I have no idea."

SHANNA SWENDSON

"I doubt you could have eaten since last night, at the earliest. I'm sure you are hungry."

"So, what is my prognosis?"

"You'll need to be careful with that cut. There are stitches in it, so no sudden moves, especially with your right arm, and don't lift anything heavy or you may tear it open. You'll be sore for some time. Otherwise, rest. Now, you sit here and drink that, and I'll check on supper."

She went back to the kitchen, where the helper had soup going in the pot and had already set places for two. "I think it's best for now if we don't let him know about the magic," Elwyn said softly. "I don't want to steal credit for your work, but we should be careful since we don't know who he is or where he's from. I'm not even sure he's telling the truth about having no memory, since there's nothing physically wrong with his head. Is dinner ready?"

The ladle scooped soup into one of the bowls. "I'll take that as a yes. I'll give you a couple of minutes before I bring him in."

Back in the sitting room, she found that her patient had finished his tea. "If you're hungry, there's soup for supper," she said.

"That sounds nice. At least, I think it does. I know what soup is, but I don't know if I like it. That's so odd." He glanced down at his bare chest. "Um, I'm not really dressed for dinner."

She handed him the shirt that the helper had cleaned and mended. "I'm afraid this was the best that could be done with this. I'll try to find you some other clothes later."

She helped him put the shirt on, then helped him get to his feet and found that he wasn't much taller than she was. He leaned on her as they walked across the hall to the kitchen, where she guided him to one of the chairs. "This seems fancy," he remarked.

It was, even fancier than usual. A vase of cut flowers—using flowers Elwyn had brought in to liven up the tea shop—had been added to the table along with the candles and tablecloth. "I like to make every meal a celebration," she said. "Even if it is simple fare. Now, enjoy."

They ate in silence for a few minutes. He didn't eat like someone who'd been starving, so she suspected he'd eaten the day before. She couldn't help but think of the last time she'd shared a meal with a man, the night her life had fallen apart. She'd stopped by Maxen's quarters to report on the status of the wounded knight, and he'd invited her to join him for dinner. That was their custom, a little charade they'd played to hide the nature of their relationship from the court. No one would have thought twice about the widowed duke having a lover, but tongues would have wagged about the healer having ensnared the duke with her wiles. It had been entirely the other way around, as she hadn't even considered that kind of relationship with him until she'd read his desire. They'd still been eating when the baron had burst in, reporting the knight's death. She'd waited for Maxen to defend her, but instead he'd looked at her with doubt and suspicion in his eyes.

The injured man broke her out of her reverie by saying, "It's awkward knowing your name but not mine."

"This is your chance to be anyone you want to be. What do you want to be called?"

He frowned in thought. "What about Bryn? That's a nice, solid name. And it rhymes with Wyn, so you should be able to remember it."

"It's nice to meet you, Bryn. You must remember something if you know names."

"I remember how to talk and eat, obviously. I suspect I'd remember how to read. It just seems that anything that might tell me who I am is a complete blank. What can you tell me about me? Surely you noticed some clues."

"You were wearing armor and had a sword on your belt."

"So I must be a knight."

"Possibly." She decided to stick to facts and not share her speculations. It was best if whatever memories that came back to him were untainted by suggestions. That way, they could be more certain that what he remembered about himself was true.

She noticed that his bowl was empty and got up to refill it. She was so accustomed to the helper doing that for her that it was unusual to see an empty bowl. She spilled some soup as it sloshed from the ladle. Clearly, she needed more practice at this. She topped off her own bowl before resuming her seat.

He grinned. "I like the idea of being a knight. Did I look dashing in the armor?"

"I was too worried about the bleeding, unconscious man I found in my garden to consider how dashing you looked in the armor." She did think that he looked rather attractive now that he was awake. He had a glint of humor in his eyes and a disarming smile.

"I wonder what else I know," he said. "I can identify the vegetables in this soup. It's seasoned with thyme, isn't it?"

Elwyn had brought in thyme, so she assumed the helper had used it. She took a quick taste to be certain before saying, "You got that correct." With a smile of her own, she said, "Perhaps you're a cook."

"There's no shame in that. Maybe I should make lunch

tomorrow so we can find out. That shouldn't be too strenuous."

"As long as you stir with your left hand."

He waved first his left hand, then his right, wincing at the motion of the right hand. "Am I right-handed or left-handed?"

"The way you wore the sword, it looked like you're right-handed, but I've known left-handed men who fought right-handed."

"The better test, then, would be to give me pen and paper and see which hand I use. Assuming I know how to write."

"After dinner, I'll get you a book and pen and paper, and we'll test your literacy."

"I hope I'm literate. Surely the fact that this matters to me means I am."

They finished their soup, and Elwyn wondered where dessert was, then remembered that the helper wasn't showing itself. She had to get up and get the cakes left over from the tea shop. She'd so quickly become spoiled by having someone to do everything for her. She found where the cakes had been wrapped in a tea towel on the sideboard and brought them to the table. "I hope these aren't too stale," she said as she served him. "The baker sometimes brings her unsold items over, and these are a couple of days old."

"Seems fine to me," he said after taking a bite.

She set a pot of mint tea to brew before she ate her own cake. Lucina's baked goods did stay fresher longer than she would have expected, now that she thought about it.

When she poured the tea, he took a long, deep sniff of his. "I think I remember liking mint," he said. "At least, I like this smell, and I know it's mint." After a sip, he said, "It's so strange not knowing anything about myself."

"Your memory likely will come back to you in time. Sometimes, when someone's been through a frightening experience, the mind just shuts down. It may be trying to protect you by keeping you from reliving what happened when you were injured."

"But why does it also have to blot out everything else?"

"Maybe you were injured because of who you are, so that's part of the pain."

"So it must have been an enemy who injured me, not some random assailant. I wonder what I was doing in your garden. You said you don't think I was wounded here?"

"I didn't hear a fight, and I'm a light sleeper. No one else around here noticed any noise. The area didn't look disturbed. But it's odd, you were in the back garden, so you must have come around the house."

"I seem to recall that people often come to each other's back doors in the country, so I might have been hoping to find help. You're a healer. That might explain why I came here. Is there a sign?"

"I don't work as a healer. The sign is for a tea shop."

"I must have been desperate for a cup of tea."

"A good cup of tea will cure a lot of things, but it doesn't help much with wounds."

"Then I'm lucky I stumbled upon a purveyor of teas who also knows how to treat wounds. I'm sure there's a story there." He grinned. "I think it's safe to say that I didn't come to burgle you during the night."

"Why not?"

"Armor would be a terrible choice of attire for a burglar. It's impossible to sneak around while wearing that stuff."

"True. You'd wake up the house with all the clanking."

"Was there any insignia on the armor?"

"None that I saw."

"May I look at it?"

"It's still in the hall."

He shoved back his seat, started to stand, then winced and put a hand to his upper chest. After a long, slow breath, he moved more gingerly until he was almost upright. "I'll have to be more careful about that." He moved haltingly out the door and to the end of the hall, by the back door. Elwyn lifted the pieces of armor for him to examine. "None of this looks familiar to me," he said, shaking his head.

She held out the sword belt, and he pulled the sword from its scabbard. He used his right hand, but he quickly had to support the sword with his left hand, as well. "Nothing on the sword to indicate who I am, either," he said. "I don't even know if this is a good sword."

He swayed, and she reached to grab the sword before he dropped it. "You've been up long enough. You should sit down."

"I thought you said I wasn't hurt too badly."

"You lost a fair amount of blood. It will take time for you to recover your strength." She set the sword down, took his elbow, and helped him toward the sitting room, where a second chair had been added in front of the fire. She guided him to one of the chairs and lowered him into it.

"Wasn't there only one chair in here before?" he asked.

"You must not have noticed the other," she said. "You were a bit foggy." The helper had clearly been busy while they were eating. Not only had it found a chair, probably in the spare room upstairs, but it had lit the candles and set out lace doilies on every horizontal surface.

"Hmm, I was so sure. Nice place you have here. Very dainty."

"The decor is all from the previous resident."

"You know, while we were trying to figure out who I am, we never addressed my earlier question. Where am I?"

Elwyn sighed before saying, "To be perfectly honest, I'm not entirely sure other than that the village is called Rydding."

"Did you wake up in the garden one day without knowing how you got there?"

"No, but I did take a small lane that turned off the road, and I found myself here without knowing exactly where I was. It's not much of a village, and it's mostly empty."

"How long have you been here?"

"About a month, I think."

He raised an eyebrow. "You think?"

"The days blur together when they're more or less the same."

"So you just stumbled into this place, as well, only without the injury, and you don't know how long you've been here. That's interesting, don't you think?"

"It does seem to be that sort of place, one you find when you need it." She noticed him wincing and shifting uncomfortably. "And you need more willow bark tea. You sit right there, I'll go make it."

"Can you leave me with a book, so I can see if I can read?"

She handed him the novel. "This was in the house when I got here. It's actually quite engrossing. Don't lose my place."

The kettle was already on the fire in the kitchen, so she took the opportunity to hurry upstairs and see what the helper was up to. She didn't know where to put Bryn for the night, and if the helper was already rearranging furniture, she wouldn't have been surprised to find that it had set up the spare room. She wasn't sure he'd be able to climb the steep stairs, though, as weak as he was.

It seemed the helper had been thinking along the same lines, for there was a pallet rolled up with linens, a pillow, and a blanket on the pile. "Good thinking," she said, keeping her voice soft enough that it wouldn't carry downstairs. "I'll put him in the sitting room for the night. And no matchmaking. He doesn't know who he is, and I'm not interested in getting involved with anyone, let alone a total stranger of unknown origins."

She carried the bedding downstairs to the sitting room. "You shouldn't try to climb those stairs, so I've got bedding to set you up down here," she said. "And now the tea should be done." As she'd expected, the helper had already brewed it, and she brought a cup to him to drink while she made up the bed.

"I appreciate all the effort you're going to for me," he said. "I'm afraid I can't pay. At least, I don't know if I can pay. For all I know, I have great piles of treasure back at home, but since I don't know where that is, I have nothing."

"There's no worry about payment. I help those in need of help, and I've recently been the recipient of great kindness, so I'm obliged to pass that on as well as I can."

"I won't impose on you for too long."

She turned from her work and looked back toward him. "But where would you go? You have nothing, and you don't know where your home is. You should stay here until you're back on your feet, at the very least. If you don't want to stay with me, much of the village is empty, and you should be able to find a place to stay, but I think you should stay here until your wound has healed a little more."

He leaned back in the chair. "You're probably right. I don't feel up to caring for myself at the moment. On the bright side, I do know how to read. I know that's not entirely common." He yawned. "I'll have to test my writing ability some other time. I know I've only been awake a little more than an hour, but I could fall asleep now."

"You need to rest. No worries about being lazy until that wound begins to heal and you get your strength back."

When he finished drinking the tea, she directed him toward the privy, then finished setting up his bed. He returned, and she helped him get down to the pallet on the floor. "I'll take another look at the wound before you go to sleep." He pulled off his boots before lying down, then she lifted his shirt and removed the bandage. "It's too soon to be showing signs of healing, but it's not festering," she reported. "It does seem to have stopped bleeding, which is good. Take care that you don't open the wound again." She dropped in more tincture and applied a fresh bandage, wrapping it under his shirt rather than undressing him.

She resisted the urge to pull up the covers and tuck him in. It was an odd urge, one she'd never felt before. She wasn't the maternal type and had never been one to want to fuss over a man, not even any of her patients. Maxen had servants to care for him and wasn't the sort of man who wanted to be tended by a woman. She stood abruptly and took a step back. "I'll have to see if I can find some clean clothes for you tomorrow. There aren't many men in the village, but there might have been some clothing left behind."

"I wonder if it's a good idea to let people know I'm here. What if the person who wounded me comes looking for me?"

"There are people here I trust to keep it quiet, and as small as the population here is, it will be difficult to keep the secret. People would at the very least notice I'm getting more food. Shall I put out the candles?"

"I can't keep my eyes open to read, so you might as well. Thank you," he said with a yawn. She took one of the candles and snuffed the others, then went up to her own room. The helper had been busy up there, as well. A small hand mirror lay on top of the nightstand. Elwyn turned it over before setting down her candle, then paused, turned back, and picked it up. She hadn't seen her face other than reflected in water or windows since she left the palace, and she was afraid of what she'd see, but she also wanted a sense of what Bryn saw.

Her face wasn't as gaunt as she'd feared it would be, though her cheeks were more hollow than they'd been before she'd fled court. Her eyes looked very dark in her pale face, and the light was too dim for her to tell if there were now any strands of white in her dark hair. She'd once been considered beautiful, elegant, and refined. Now she wasn't sure how she'd describe herself. Striking, perhaps, if the beholder could get past her shabby clothing.

Not that it mattered. She wasn't looking for romance, and especially not with a man who didn't know who he was. He might have a wife and children back home. Or he could be a villain. He seemed nice, but she didn't know how he'd come to be wounded. She'd help heal his wound and look after him until he knew where to go, but that was it.

She just hoped whoever had wounded him didn't come looking for him. She had enough to worry about with her own enemies without having to worry about his.

CHAPTER 7

Bryn was still asleep when Elwyn came downstairs the next morning. She tiptoed past the sitting room into the kitchen so she wouldn't disturb him. After a quick breakfast, she dashed off a note to let him know she was running errands and left the pen and ink with it, in case he wanted to see if he could write. The helper arranged bread on a plate with a pot of honey nearby. "Remember, don't let him know you're there," Elwyn warned. "And no doilies. I don't want him to think I'd put out such a thing." She got the distinct impression of an insulted sniff, even though she heard nothing.

She headed to the village center, where the market was in progress. She wouldn't be able to talk properly to Mair while others were around, but she needed more food with another mouth to feed. She was able to trade some fresh herbs for more lentils, and the Chicken Lady offered her extra eggs with a sly wink that made Elwyn wonder if she'd seen something. The miller wasn't there, and she assumed he wasn't feeling up to standing in the market yet. Her medicines were good, but not that miraculous.

When the customers in the market had thinned out, she got close to Mair and said softly, "Do you know of anyone who has men's clothing to spare?" Before her friend could respond with something ribald, she added, "Quiet! This is serious."

"If you have an unclothed man, it's definitely serious," Mair said with a grin, though she did keep her voice down.

"He's a patient," Elwyn said. "His own shirt was damaged when he was wounded. I want to see if I can find something fresh for him."

"What size is he?"

"Not much taller than I am. Lean."

"Some of my brother's things should fit him. But you'll have to tell me the whole story about how you came to have a patient who doesn't have spare clothes of his own handy."

"When we're not in the market."

"Oh, sounds serious."

"It may be."

"Well, I've almost sold all the milk and cream. As soon as I get home, I'll see what I can find and bring it over."

"Or I could come pick it up."

"You don't want me to meet him."

"Not yet. It would do you no good, anyway. He's not up to strenuous activity."

"Well, in that case, I can wait to meet him. Or are you saving him for yourself?"

"He's a patient. And I am a professional."

"Come by before lunch. But the whole story, mind you. I want details about how he got here and who he is."

Bryn was awake and eating breakfast in the kitchen when Elwyn returned from the market. She normally would have handed her purchases over to the helper, but she couldn't do that in front of him, so she took them to the pantry, where the helper could deal with them out of sight. "Good news!" Bryn greeted her when she returned from the pantry.

"You remember who you are?"

"Alas, no. The news isn't that good. But it does appear that I know how to write. If you need anything written, I'm your man." With a rueful smile, he added, "I'm afraid I'm not good for much else at the moment." He shoved her note over to her. On the back of it, he'd copied the note. His handwriting was much better than hers.

"How do you feel about making labels?" she asked.

"Put me to work!"

"Finish your breakfast first. Then I want to get a look at that wound. How does it feel?"

"Sore. Better if I move very gingerly and barely move my right arm."

"Then you might not want to do a lot of writing. Give it at least another day. The labels can wait. Any headache or dizziness? Does the wound feel warm?"

"No headache, just that bruise on my face, which is throbbing. I feel weak and unsteady if I'm up for too long."

"Then don't stay up for too long," she couldn't resist teasing. "I can put something on that bruise that should help." It had developed into a dark blue, and some of the blue had spread into the hollow under his eye. She took a salve from the stash in the pantry and brought it to him. "Turn your cheek toward me and hold still," she instructed before dabbing the salve on as gently as she could. He winced and hissed in pain at her touch, but otherwise managed to remain still. "Now, let's get a look at that wound."

"Do you need me to lie down?"

"Not unless you need to." She lifted his shirt and unwound the bandage, then pulled the linen pad away from the wound. "No redness. That's good," she reported. She dropped more tincture on it, then put a fresh bandage on and wound the cloth on to secure it before pulling his shirt back into place.

"So I'm going to live?"

"You'll survive this particular incident. I can't promise anything else. Now, back to the sitting room with you so I can tidy the kitchen and start work on lunch." She helped him stand and got him across the hall. "Would you rather sit in the chair or lie down?"

"The chair. I'm not sleepy yet. Do you mind if I read your book?"

"As long as you don't lose my place. I'll make you some more willow bark tea. That should help with the discomfort." She got back to the kitchen to find that the helper had already tidied up from breakfast and had put the previous night's soup on to reheat. The kettle was bubbling, so she brewed the willow bark tea. "I'm going to Mair's for some clothes," she whispered to the helper. "And I'm sure you've already found what I got at the market. I'll tackle the garden when I get back."

She brought the tea to Bryn and said, "I have some more errands to run, but I shouldn't be away long."

"I'm sure I can survive," he said dryly.

"Just don't do anything that would tear open those stitches."

"Have no fear. It hurts enough before I even get to that point."

Mair was home from the market and unloading her cart when Elwyn arrived at the dairy. Before Elwyn even reached her, Mair said, "Now, you have to tell me why you need men's clothing." She grabbed Elwyn's arm and marched her into the house.

"Well, remember what you said about men falling out of the sky and into your garden?"

"That didn't happen!"

"I doubt he fell from the sky, but I did find him in my garden. He'd been injured, and I patched him up, but his shirt was torn and bloody."

"What happened to him? Where did he come from? And, most important, is he handsome?"

"I don't know what happened, and neither does he. That's the odd thing. He doesn't remember who he is, but he doesn't have a head injury. As for handsome, I suppose he might be, especially when he smiles."

Mair grinned. "It sounds like you've claimed him, then, if you're noticing his smile."

"It's a nice smile," Elwyn admitted, feeling her face grow warm.

"I suppose I'll have to wait for the next man who falls out of the sky." Mair led her up the stairs to one of the rooms, which looked disused. The mattress on the bed was bare. Mair opened a chest and dug around, then handed Elwyn a shirt. "Do you think this would fit?"

Elwyn held the shirt against herself and said, "I think so." Then, hoping she wasn't getting into painful territory, she said tentatively, "You never mentioned a brother."

"He's been gone a long time. Like so much of the rest of the village."

Elwyn couldn't tell if that meant he'd left or was dead, or something else, but Mair looked uncharacteristically serious, so she dropped the subject.

"Does he need other clothes?"

"All he has is a shirt and breeches. He was wearing armor over that."

"Armor? Really? So a knight in shining armor with a nice smile landed in your garden. Some women have all the luck."

"I'm not sure I'd call it lucky, since I don't know who he is. He may be a terrible person. Or he may have a family back home."

"And you're alone in your house with him?"

"Well, not entirely alone. And he's not moving very quickly, so I think I'm perfectly safe for the time being. If he hasn't regained his memory by the time he's healed, I may suggest that he find a house in the village to move into."

"That sounds like a good plan. Then he'll be fair game for the rest of us. Here are some breeches and a jacket. Oh, and he'll want clean socks." She handed a bundle of clothing to Elwyn.

"Thank you."

"It's not as though anyone was using them, but there's been no one to give them to." Mair grinned. "Maybe whatever it is that draws people here heard my pleas and has started bringing us men."

"I'm more concerned with what happened near enough to the village that a wounded man was able to make it to my cottage."

"Is that why you asked me about hearing something?"

"I don't think he was hurt in my garden, but the person who hurt him may be close by. My patient couldn't have gone far in his condition."

"That is troubling."

"I'd best get back to him. Thank you for the clothes. And since we don't know who might be looking for him, I'd appreciate it if we could keep this between us."

"Your secret is safe with me. Mostly because I have no one to talk to other than you and Lucina."

"And everyone else in the market."

"I don't talk about anything truly important with anyone but you and Lucina. But I won't tell her."

Elwyn sighed. "I may have to tell her, since I'll need more bread. It will be hard to keep people from noticing there's an extra person at the house for long."

Mair escorted her down the stairs and outside. She took a wedge of cheese from the cart and handed it to Elwyn. "Here's my contribution. It didn't sell today, so I might as well give it to you. But when he's feeling better, I want to meet him."

"If he agrees."

Elwyn crossed the road back to her cottage and found Bryn dozing in a chair, the book lying on his lap. She laid the clothes on the other chair and slipped out of the room to bring the cheese to the kitchen. While she waited for him to wake up for lunch, she went outside to see to the garden. She inspected it thoroughly for any signs that the fight that had injured Bryn could have taken place nearby, but she didn't see any trampled plants or disturbed ground. The only footprints she saw must have been his, but they were only visible from near the edge of the garden, under the trees, to where she'd found him. She couldn't see how he'd come to that place because either the ground was too firm or any plants he'd trampled had sprung back since then.

"Where is it that you found me?" Bryn's voice startled her, but she fought to hide her reaction before she turned around. He was dressed in the clean clothes, which were only a bit too big for him, and she thought he looked stronger and steadier.

"Over there," she said, pointing. "I can't see any sign of which direction you came from."

"Could I have been dumped?"

"There are a few footprints just before you fell, and they aren't deep enough to have been someone carrying you, so I think you got here on your own."

He glanced in both directions. "So, either from the road, or from that direction." He pointed toward the back of the garden. "What's back there?"

"There's a footpath that follows the brook past the mill and then up toward the castle."

He shaded his eyes with his hand and squinted into the distance toward the castle. "Is the lord in residence? It looks like his flag is flying." He turned to her and grinned. "Hey, I know that much. Maybe I am a knight."

"The villagers claim they haven't seen or heard from the lord in years. Given that he's made no attempt to collect rents, I'm inclined to believe them. He must have left when everyone else did and didn't bother to lower his flag. Or someone went up there and raised the flag to make it look like the castle is occupied." She didn't share her thought about him having been held prisoner there because she didn't want to plant a potential false memory.

"What do you know about him?"

"Nothing. Not even his name or title, now that I think about it. They tend not to bother with names much around here. It's just 'the brook,' 'the lane,' 'the lord,' and 'the castle.' As though there's only one, so there's no point in complicating matters."

"If you don't mind, I'd like to look around out here, in case something jogs my memory," he said.

"Just don't overdo it."

"No worries of that," he said with a wince.

"I'll be inside. I'd better see to lunch."

"I won't be long."

Him being outside was a relief, because it allowed the helper to get lunch on the table without Elwyn having to fumble through the tasks. The soup had been dished neatly into bowls, with bread and slices of Mair's cheese on plates beside them. He came in soon afterward and waited for Elwyn to sit before he took his own seat. "Nothing," he reported with a sigh. "As far as I can tell, I've never seen anything around here in any direction. It's odd feeling so utterly blank."

"You need more time to recover."

"What if I never get my memory back?"

"Then you have a blank slate to start your life over again. You can decide who and what you want to be." She had to admit, the thought was appealing. If she knew she would have her needs met, that she would have a way to make a living and a place to live, she might wish for that, herself. It would be nice to put her past completely behind her and start over again. It would be dangerous, though, because her enemies wouldn't forget her, and not knowing them would leave her vulnerable. That was his situation, she realized. Someone had injured him, and he had no way of knowing who it was. Anyone he encountered could be the person who'd fought him.

"But what am I leaving behind? Are there people who depend on me? Is someone looking for me or thinking I abandoned them? That's the main reason I want to know. It would be good to know whether I have a home to go to. Don't you have to know what past you're escaping to want to escape your past?"

"That is true. Losing your past should be an option you get to choose, not one forced upon you."

"Though I suppose you wouldn't know you had chosen it, unless you left yourself a note. My past couldn't have been ideal if someone attacked me."

"However, escaping your past would keep you from resolving the problems that made you want to escape it in the first place. They'd still be there, maybe getting worse."

"In other words, I can't fix what's wrong if I don't know what it is. Very wise."

"But there's nothing you can do about it now except rest and try to get better, and maybe your memory will return."

After lunch, he insisted on trying to write labels, so she gave him a scribbled list of the names she needed on labels, some squares of paper, pen, and ink. She sat beside him at the table, mixing herbs and putting them in jars. They worked together mostly in silence, but it was a comfortable, companionable silence. She didn't feel like he was intruding on her. His presence was almost as restful as being alone. When it came time to put the labels on the jars, she got out the glue pot, and she was surprised when he automatically reached for the right jar to go with the label he'd just smeared glue on.

"How did you know that?" she asked.

"Know what?"

"That's the right label. You must know something about herbs."

He blinked and looked at the jar and the label. "I suppose I do." She quizzed him on the rest, and he got them right. The only ones that stumped him were her personal blends. Next, she tested him on their uses, and he knew that, too.

"You must be an herbalist, yourself. Or an apothecary."

"Which doesn't fit with the armor and sword, unless

perhaps I'm a battlefield healer. I may have the armor and sword to protect me, but my main job is to care for injuries or the sort of illnesses that come up in camps. But why would someone want to hurt the healer? Have there been any battles nearby?"

"No armies have marched through here since I've been here, and I wasn't aware there was any war. The kingdom was at peace, last I heard."

"Perhaps it was a training exercise." He grinned. "And I made someone angry by winning too many hands of cards." He put the last label on a jar and said, "Is there anything else you need me to do? Because if not, I believe I'll take a nap and hope I wake up with my memory intact."

"That sounds like a good idea. I'll be out front in the shop." She shut the sitting room door after he entered so she wouldn't disturb his rest, then carried all the jars out to the shop and arranged them on the shelves. There weren't a lot of customers that afternoon, for which she was grateful. She wouldn't have been able to give them her full attention.

The question of what this village was continued to nag at her. Surely the former inhabitants of the cottage would have known if there was something odd about this area. Mother Dilys should have recorded when people left or disappeared. That was one of the duties of the healer. Elwyn had resisted looking for the logbook because having it in her possession would mean she was accepting the role, making a commitment. As long as she didn't have the book, she could tell herself she was merely recommending herbal remedies while living in the cottage. No one but the resident healer was supposed to look at the book. Everything recorded there was private, and reading it without being the healer would mean she was prying.

On the other hand, she couldn't continue to recommend remedies responsibly without knowing the histories of the local people. She needed to know if someone had reacted badly to a particular herb and what chronic conditions she should look out for. She also thought that knowing more about this place might help her know more about what had happened to Bryn.

So, she needed to find that logbook. She knew it wasn't in the sitting room, pantry, or shop. She went up to her room and dug through the chest, looking under all the linens. "Do you know where the book is?" she asked the helper. A clatter from the spare room answered her.

The helper had made good progress in organizing the room. It had revealed the bed, but the room wasn't quite ready for occupancy. A stack of boxes slid off a chest against the far wall, and she went over there and opened the chest. Inside she found a great quantity of lace doilies, some faded paper flowers, and underneath it all was a large, crudely bound book that had more doilies pasted on it. She could barely lift it out of the chest.

"Now, let's see what you can tell me about where I am," she said as she carried it toward the window.

CHAPTER 8

The first page in the book established that this cottage had initially been built more than a hundred and fifty years ago, and the first resident had been a Mother Gladys. "Gladys? Is that who you are?" Elwyn asked, and was answered by a cheerful flutter of the lace curtains. "You had lovely penmanship, Gladys." The ink had faded to a reddish brown, but the perfectly even lettering with plenty of swirls and flourishes was still quite legible.

As curious as Elwyn was about Gladys, the events of more than a century ago probably wouldn't pertain to her current situation, so she flipped to the back. The last entry recorded Mother Dilys's departure, more than five years ago. "As I am departing because there isn't enough work to keep me busy, I am leaving the cottage without a replacement," the entry read. "I trust that when a new healer is needed, she'll find her way here." The entries before that were sparse, showing why she felt she wasn't busy enough. She saw barely one patient a week toward the end.

Elwyn noted that the miller had a history of stomach woes. It seemed he liked to harvest wild mushrooms, and he wasn't good at telling the difference between the ones that were edible and the ones that would make him ill. He did, at least, know to avoid the truly dangerous ones. Mother Dilys had administered the same preparations Elwyn had given him. Perhaps what he really needed was a lesson on foraging mushrooms, Elwyn thought.

The log also mentioned when people gave up and left town—the innkeeper, the brewer, and others. They all left because they didn't have enough customers to stay in business. But why had people gone before that?

There was an entry from about ten years ago that read as though it had been written in some confusion, a mention that Dilys could have sworn that there had been more people in the village, and no one had seen the lord. It was as though a large percentage of the population had simply vanished, but people weren't certain they had ever been there. It reminded Elwyn of the way Mair had talked about her brother—she seemed to be sure she had one, since she had his belongings, but she didn't know what had happened to him. She also had sounded foggy about her past, with a vague sense that she'd danced with someone once, though she wasn't entirely sure.

It all sounded to Elwyn as though the village was under some kind of spell, or perhaps the lord had been cursed and that had somehow extended to the whole village. That was far beyond her area of expertise. She had the ability to sense what others were feeling, but real magic was quite beyond her. They'd need a wizard to tackle this problem. This also didn't seem to have anything to do with Bryn, unless whoever had cursed the lord was living in his castle and holding people prisoner there. Would they find the missing townspeople in the castle? She couldn't imagine that no one had ever looked, unless there was something keeping them out.

She'd been reluctant to introduce Mair to Bryn, but maybe she should. Mair might recognize him if he turned out to be one of the missing townspeople. She had a feeling she wouldn't have to wait long for that. If she knew Mair, she wouldn't be able to resist coming over to meet the newcomer.

In the meantime, she took the book to her room, sat at the small desk there, and dutifully recorded that she had assumed possession of the cottage, though she wasn't sure of the precise date. Then she tried to remember the people she'd given any kind of treatment and the results she knew of. She left Bryn out, for the moment. She didn't want a written record of him until she knew more about his situation. Her recordkeeping complete, she locked the book up inside her desk and went downstairs, feeling like she had more of a mystery than before, and no real answers other than what was ailing the miller.

Then it was time to open the shop. As she'd expected, Mair dropped by with some fresh milk not long afterward. "I had extra and thought you could offer it with tea," she said.

"He's still resting," Elwyn said with a smile.

Mair sat at a table and said, "I'm in no rush. I'll have a cup of that spicy blend."

"That sounds good." Both women turned to see Bryn standing in the doorway. "I'm sorry, I didn't mean to intrude. I heard voices, and I was thirsty."

A smile spread slowly across Mair's face, as though she liked what she saw. Elwyn was surprised by the surge of jealousy that rushed through her. It wasn't as though she wanted him for herself, so it was silly for her to be jealous over Mair's appreciation of Bryn. It didn't look like Mair recognized him, though. There went the theory that he was one of the missing villagers. "Mair, this is my guest, Bryn," Elwyn said. "Bryn, Mair is my neighbor. She runs the dairy and keeps me supplied with milk and cheese."

"Pleased to meet you," Mair said.

"Likewise," he said with a slight bow of his head. "I've been enjoying your cheese."

"Come join us for tea," Mair said.

He turned toward Elwyn, as though asking permission. She nodded, and he took a seat at Mair's table.

Mair gave him an appraising glance. "You seem to be healing nicely. And you look very nice in those clothes."

"The clothes were Mair's brother's," Elwyn explained. "She lent them."

"I thank you, lady," he said. "You came to my aid in my hour of need."

Elwyn bit the inside of her lip to keep herself from smiling. She wasn't sure if he was mocking Mair or merely playing along. He seemed to have decided to go with the idea that he was a knight. If only Mair had seen him labeling herb jars earlier. "Your color does seem to be better," she said. "Is the pain easing?"

"Somewhat," he said. "I don't feel quite as stiff. I still won't be swinging a sword anytime soon."

"And you don't remember anything about who you are?" Mair asked.

"Nothing, I'm afraid."

"This is such a fascinating mystery. Exciting things like this don't happen around here."

"Which is part of the mystery," Elwyn said. "What happened, and why here?"

"This village does seem to draw people to it. How long do you think he could have lasted with that wound?"

"I don't know. It wasn't too deep, so it wasn't damaging any vital organs. The main problem was blood loss. He might have come from as far as the main road before collapsing."

"Should we go out there and check?" Mair suggested. "Maybe the other guy is there."

"Seeing the location might spark a memory," Bryn said.

"No, I don't think you're up to walking that far," Elwyn said.

"I have a cart and a horse," Mair said. "Tomorrow after I've made my rounds, I'll drop by and pick you up. Depending on how far we have to go, we should be able to be back before it's time to open the shop, but you can always open a bit later. Business hours around here are understood to be somewhat fluid."

Elwyn was uneasy with the plan, but she could think of no more objections. There weren't too many people out and about on this end of the village, so no one was likely to see a man leaving her cottage and getting into a cart. Bryn could be right that seeing the path he must have taken might spur his memories.

The next morning, she and Bryn went out to meet Mair. "I packed a picnic lunch, so we can make a day of it," Mair said cheerfully as she pulled up in front of the cottage. "Now, hop in back."

Elwyn helped Bryn into the cart and said, "I'll walk ahead. I don't think anyone's come this way since Bryn arrived, so I may be able to spot any footprints."

"Good thinking." Mair clicked her tongue, and her old cart horse began plodding forward. Elwyn didn't have to walk too quickly to stay ahead of it. This stretch of road was fairly dry, and there hadn't been any rain since Bryn arrived, so footprints didn't show up. They reached the edge of the forest, the tunnel of trees Elwyn had emerged from at her lowest point to see the village ahead of her. She realized she was hesitating, afraid to step past that threshold. If the village was truly enchanted, would she be able to find it again? Would it still be there when she came out of the trees?

She supposed that meant that she actually wanted to be there if she wanted to be able to go back. On the other hand, she didn't have her purse or her belongings with her, so if she was stranded outside the village, she'd be worse off than she had been when she first stumbled upon it. However, she wouldn't be alone. That was some consolation. Mair being with her would probably allow them to return, anyway, since she was from the village, and if the village had drawn Elwyn to be a healer there, surely it would allow her to return. She was glad she'd accepted the book, which made her tie to the cottage official. Even so, she realized she was holding her breath as she crossed the threshold of the trees until she turned back and could still see the village behind her. She breathed out in a happy sigh, smiling to herself at the childish flight of fancy.

The ground was softer in the shade, as it never got the chance to fully dry. "I see footprints!" she called out. "Looks like they're heading toward the village. They seem to be about the right size."

"So, I did come this way," Bryn said. "But when, and from where?"

They hadn't gone much farther when Elwyn noticed a cut in the side of a tree—a fresh one, the wood still showing raw under the bark. "Stop!" she said. "This may be it. See that tree?" The cut would have been at just the right height for someone to have swung at Bryn's neck.

"They must have been trying to take my head off," he said, rubbing at his neck. "Obviously, I ducked or got out of the way. Or I was swinging at them and I missed."

"Your sword didn't look like it had chopped into a tree," Elwyn said. "There's another cut over there. The ground's been really stirred up around here. This has to be where the fight happened."

Bryn frowned as he surveyed the whole area. "Is anything coming to you?" Mair asked.

He shook his head. "I don't get any sense that I've ever been here before. But what happened to the other man? How many sets of footprints lead away from here?"

"Unless they perfectly matched where you stepped, there was only one set of footprints heading to the village," Elwyn said. She picked her way around the site of the fight. "There are hoofprints here—probably from more than one horse, and they seem to be leading away, back toward the road."

"So I must have scared him off," Brynn said.

"Or he left you for dead and took your horse," Mair suggested. "If you won, wouldn't you have taken your horse with you?"

"If I was barely conscious from pain and the loss of blood, I might not have been thinking clearly. I managed to stagger away and find help, and he recovered his senses to find himself alone, so he rode away with both horses."

"I'm no expert at this," Elwyn said. "All I can tell is that more than one person moved around a lot in this area, there are slash marks on a couple of the trees, there's one set of footprints heading toward the village, and there are hoof-prints leading away. Beyond that, I'm not sure you could tell." She knew of people who could magically read a scene and re-create what had occurred there, but that wasn't one of her gifts. "It looks like someone might have lain on the ground over there, near where the footprints began." She pointed to the spot where the leaves and moss had been disturbed. "There might even be some blood on the ground there. The rest of the ground is too disturbed for me to tell if a second person ever fell."

"So, we know where it must have happened, but still have no idea what happened," Mair said.

Elwyn tried opening her magical senses, which were usually only good when she had direct contact with another person, but she might sense if magic had been used nearby recently. Bryn had been touched with magic, and if magic had been used on him here, she might be able to sense it. She thought she felt a trace of something magical, but it had been days, and the forest had its own magic, so it wasn't a strong enough lead to make it worth the explanations that would be required to share it.

"Help me down," Bryn said. "Maybe if I retrace my steps, something will come back to me." He and Elwyn walked past the location of the fight so he could approach it the way he must have. They reached the fight spot once more, and he walked around that whole area, then followed his footsteps toward the edge of the forest, before turning back around and sighing heavily. "Nothing. None of this is familiar. As far as I can tell, I've never been here before. Maybe this wasn't me, after all." He looked down and added, "Though the prints do seem to match my boots."

"Now what?" Mair asked. "We didn't get as far as I expected. Where shall we have our picnic? There's a nice little bridge not far from here. We can sit on the side of it."

Since it wasn't far, Bryn stayed out of the cart and

walked with Elwyn, taking her arm and leaning slightly on her. "This is very frustrating," he said.

"I can imagine. It must be disconcerting not knowing who you are."

"At the moment, I'm more concerned about the fact that there's someone out there who wants to hurt me, and I don't know if they're justified. What if I'm the villain here?"

"I find that hard to imagine."

"But you don't know me or what I'm really like. I don't even know that. Maybe I'm only reasonably nice because I don't remember all the things that make me a terrible person."

"I think this situation has shown something of who you really are when everything else is stripped away, and you seem to be kind and intelligent. If you were acting as a villain, then you must have been miserable as you acted against your instincts." A shiver of unease went through her as she realized that was exactly what she'd been doing for nearly a decade. Not that she'd been a villain, but she'd run away from her old life and her mother's dreams for her to follow her calling as a healer, and then she'd left a life of helping ordinary people to be a duke's personal healer and tend to people at court while she lived a life of luxury. It had seemed like a pleasant life, but she had to admit that she'd been unhappy deep down inside. "Let's just say I understand something about that."

He didn't probe, for which she was grateful. She was barely able to confess it to herself. It would take her some time to ponder this realization before she was ready to talk to anyone else about it.

They had their picnic on the very spot where Elwyn had reached her lowest point and decided she wanted to live. It was a pleasant place—not necessarily a place where she'd want to die, but a good place to sit on a warm afternoon with friends. "While we're wondering why Bryn was here," Mair said, "what brought you down this lane, Wyn?"

"I didn't want to be on the main road anymore, and this was the first lane I came across after I made that decision." Had there been something pulling on her or calling to her? It hadn't seemed like it at the time.

"I'm very glad you did," Mair said, draping an arm over Elwyn's shoulders and giving her a slight hug. "The village has become so much more fun with you here."

On Elwyn's other side, Bryn also draped his arm around her. "I'm also glad you did. I don't know what would have become of me if I'd collapsed outside an abandoned cottage."

But as much as Elwyn tried to enjoy the outing with her friends, she couldn't help but worry about why Bryn and the person he'd fought had been on the lane to the village —if that was what had happened. She couldn't think of any good reasons why a pair of armed men would come to this remote location. The main thing that came to mind was that they were looking for her. If they'd been sent by the baron, she could be aiding her own enemy.

CHAPTER 9

For the journey home, Elwyn couldn't think of a good reason why she shouldn't ride in the cart with Bryn instead of walking ahead or alongside it, but she wished she didn't have to ride in the cart with him. Thinking of him as a potential enemy changed her feelings about him.

But when she looked at him, she couldn't seem to see him as an enemy, as an assassin or investigator sent by the baron to find her. If that was what he was, he must have been miserable because without his memories he wasn't at all the sort of person who could live that kind of life. He would have been going against his essential nature. That could explain why he'd lost all memory of his identity. Perhaps he'd been recruited and trained from childhood, forced into a life he wouldn't have chosen for himself.

That was a nice story, but it was hard for her to believe. If he was an assassin, then he had to be one who operated more by stealth than by force. He didn't have the body of someone who was trained for fighting and killing. He might be able to sneak up behind someone with a knife. Or his main weapon could be poison. He did know his herbs. Was he living in her home, waiting for a chance to poison her? She doubted Gladys would let him put poison in her food or drink, but perhaps she should be careful if they were ever away from home.

Now that she thought about it, how could she even be certain that he really had lost his memory? Without knowing anything about him, she couldn't test him or try to trick him. She couldn't call out his real name and see if he instinctively responded or feed him something he was allergic to and see if he knew to refuse to eat it. Could his amnesia all be an act to make him seem harmless? He really had been wounded, so maybe he was waiting until he was healed and no longer needed her before he poisoned her.

"I seem to have staggered quite a way before I collapsed," he remarked as they emerged from the tunnel of trees.

"You weren't wounded that badly. The main problem was the loss of blood, which would have taken some time to affect you," Elwyn said.

"It must have been a moonlit night. Otherwise, I don't know how I would have made it without bumping into things." He rubbed the fading bruise on his cheek. "Or maybe I did bump into things."

"It wasn't quite a full moon, but there was some moonlight," Elwyn said.

"So I'd have been able to see your cottage. Would there have been any lights inside?"

"It depends on what time you arrived. There might have been light showing if you came before I went to bed. You were far enough from the house that I might not have heard you in the garden while I was awake."

She watched his face carefully as he considered this, but she could find no sign of artifice. There was a way she could test him, she knew. She hesitated because it was intrusive and questionable for her to do when it was merely for her benefit rather than to help him, but she had to know. She placed a gentle hand on his and said, "I'm sure it will come back to you," as she opened her senses to read him. She immediately felt a wave of confusion and frustration. He wasn't hiding anything. That didn't mean he wasn't an assassin sent to kill her, but if he was, he didn't know it.

There was one other thing she read from him: affection. Toward her? Her gift wasn't the sort that could tell her that kind of detail, but he had a warm glow of affection about him. Aside from the frustration about his identity, he was happy and balanced. She removed her hand from his before she could give in to the temptation to probe more deeply.

"I think I'm mostly worried about what I might have left behind and who might have hurt me," he said. "Otherwise, I wouldn't mind staying here. In the village, I mean."

She turned to look at him and found him looking back at her with a crooked smile. "It is a nice village," she said.

"And we'd be happy to have an extra man," Mair said with a glance back over her shoulder. Elwyn had almost forgotten she was there while she was pondering Bryn's identity.

The cart stopped in front of the cottage, and Elwyn helped Bryn down before Mair drove away. "Well, we learned one thing, maybe," Bryn said as they entered the cottage. "If that was where I was attacked, my attacker seems to have gone the other way. That's good, right? If he wanted to kill me, surely he'd know where to go and would have been here by now."

"True." If it had been one of the baron's men, Elwyn was fairly certain he wouldn't have fled. So maybe Bryn had nothing to do with that.

Bryn rested while she opened the shop, and by dinner-time he showed no ill effects from the day's exertions. He didn't want to go to sleep immediately after dinner, so Elwyn brought a couple of cups of mint tea to the sitting room, and they sat by the fire together. She wished she had some kind of needlework to do, although she'd always hated being forced by her mother to do such things, just to have something to keep herself busy. It felt strange to sit totally idle. She wrapped her hands around her teacup, just to give them something to do.

Bryn must have felt the same thing. "I have a feeling that I would normally read in a situation like this," he said. "Alas, we have but one book between us. Should I read it aloud?"

"Yes, please," she said. That would prevent them having to make conversation and she wouldn't have to worry about accidentally expressing her concerns about why he'd come this way in the first place or about what affection he might be feeling.

"I'll start where I left off, so I'm afraid it might duplicate what you've already read."

"I don't mind. It will remind me what happened before I left off. I haven't had a chance to read in days."

"I'm sorry about that. I know it's my fault, since you've had a patient who's also a house guest. You've had no chance to just sit in your own sitting room and relax." He cleared his throat and began reading. His voice was deep and pleasant, and as he read, she thought she detected a slight hint of an accent, probably from one of the northern counties. He read well, putting expression behind the words and even slightly altering his voice for each charac-ter. Elwyn closed her eyes and settled back in her chair,

93

allowing his words to conjure images in her mind. It was almost like being at the theater.

She jolted out of the spell he'd woven when he paused to take a sip of tea. "Sorry, throat got dry," he said, apparently noticing that she'd opened her eyes as though startled. "I didn't realize reading was such thirsty work."

"You do it well."

"I wonder if I'm an actor. Was the armor a costume? But I don't know why an actor would be roaming the woods in costume, far from any theater, and getting into a fight."

"A dissatisfied audience member tracked you down?"

"How dare you!" he said in mock protest. "I would never leave an audience dissatisfied."

"Would an actor be carrying a real sword, though?"

"I'm not sure. I don't feel like I know much about the theater, though I could have forgotten, given that I've forgotten everything." He drank more tea, and she tried to think of a way to lift his mood, since a dark shadow seemed to have come over his features. He recovered quickly on his own, though, smiling and saying, "It's your turn."

"For what? To read?"

"If you like. Or you could talk. Entertain me. I need to rest. Besides, I can't talk about myself because that would be a short conversation. Tell me about you. You know how to mend a wound, but you're running a tea shop. How did that happen?"

"That is a very long story."

He settled back in his chair and stretched out his legs. "I'm not going anywhere, though it is possible that I might fall asleep, especially if it's not an interesting story."

"I did train to be a healer, but I don't do that anymore because it turned out I wasn't very good at it. So now I'm using the knowledge of herbs I gained from my training to blend teas."

"That's not a very long story."

"I left out the boring parts."

"You said you happened to stumble upon this place. Where were you coming from and why were you here?"

She took a moment to consider how much to tell him. His reaction might give her a clue if it sparked some recognition in him. "I had left my previous job due to that issue of not being very good at it and was just wandering until I found a place I could stay. I thought of the idea of a tea shop when Mair was having tea with me in the kitchen. A healer used to live in this house, so the garden is full of herbs."

"You're holding out on me, Wyn," he said with a grin. "There's got to be a story of passion and intrigue. Let's see, you're a runaway heiress who took refuge in a cottage in the woods, where you learned the trade of a healer, until a handsome nobleman happened by and offered you a position in his court and fell in love with you, but the romance went wrong, and you ran away again to find this cottage, where you live simply."

She shivered with the awareness of how close he'd come to the truth. How had he done that? Maybe she wasn't the only one with an ability to read people. "I'm afraid it's not that exciting," she said.

He yawned, then hurried to say, "I wasn't agreeing with you about it not being exciting. I just may be more tired than I realized after today's excursion."

She stood and took his cup from him. "Then I will leave you to get some rest. Perhaps one more night down here. Then I'll get the spare room ready in case you feel up to climbing stairs. That might be more comfortable than sleeping on the floor."

"The floor isn't that uncomfortable."

She paused in the doorway on her way out. "Good night."

"Good night, Wyn." The way he said her name and looked at her made her grow warm. She felt almost as though he was looking through her, and she couldn't help but wonder what she'd feel if she touched him and read his emotions. She hurried to the stairs so she wouldn't be tempted to do so.

As she got ready for bed, she considered that she'd actually enjoyed the evening. Not the part in which she'd had to discuss her past, but it had been refreshing to have a man actually interested in hearing about her. She didn't think the duke had ever asked her anything about her past. Her role had been to listen while he talked about his day and the problems he was wrestling with and occasionally ask him questions to help him consider different angles. He'd never asked her what she'd done, other than updates on patients who mattered to him. Maybe he should have lost his memory so he'd have had less to talk about, she mused with a smile.

The next morning, Bryn was livelier than she'd ever seen him. He claimed not to be in pain, and he clearly had more energy. It seemed he'd turned the corner. That meant that when he invited himself along on her trip to the market, she didn't have a good reason to tell him he couldn't come, other than the caution that it might be dangerous to reveal his presence, in case the person who'd wounded him was looking for him.

"I could also encounter someone who recognizes me and can tell me who I am," he said. "I can't hide out in your house forever. People are going to learn about my presence sooner or later if this village is as small as you say it is."

She supposed it was his problem if the person he encountered was an enemy. She had tended to his wound but had no authority over him. She couldn't make him stay home. "Very well, then. Come along. But I can assure you, there's not much to the market."

It turned out that the market was actually a bit larger than usual, since the miller, apparently having recovered from his stomach woes, was there, and there was a peddler Elwyn hadn't seen before. The Chicken Lady had staked out her usual spot, from which she spewed insults at the peddler, much to Mair's amusement.

"This seems a lively scene," Bryn remarked.

"That's a new peddler," Elwyn said softly to him as they approached the market. "Perhaps you should stay away." She wondered if she should avoid the market, herself, since she didn't know what the baron might be doing in his search for her. Sending one of his men to prowl villages in the disguise of a peddler would probably require more imagination than he had, but she couldn't afford to lower her guard.

But it was too late for her to avoid attention, as the Chicken Lady shouted, "I have some eggs for you, girlie, and I could use your help!"

"What help do you need?" she asked the Chicken Lady as she drew nearer. She'd yet to learn the woman's name, and she wasn't sure that anyone else knew it. Even Mair called her the Chicken Lady.

"I've got this tickle in me throat," the woman said, scratching the scarf wound around her neck.

"Do you have a cough? Does it hurt to swallow?"

"It's just a tickle."

"Any warm drink may help it, then, preferably with

honey. I can bring something over to you later. I don't have the right thing with me now."

"I could go get it," Bryn offered.

"Are you sure you're up to it?"

"I feel fine. The sage?"

"Yes. And I think some of the cold blend, just in case." She asked the woman, "Do you have honey?"

"Yes, I trade eggs for it."

To Bryn, Elwyn said, "That should do it. Three days worth of each." He nodded and headed off. She found it interesting that he knew just what was needed. She'd never met a male healer, but she didn't know if that was because the gift was exclusively feminine or if it was merely that most men weren't inclined to that sort of work. It didn't fit with the armor and sword, unless perhaps he'd served as a battlefield medic, as he'd speculated.

Once he was gone, she checked with the miller. "How are you feeling?" she asked.

"Much better. I've even managed to eat regular meals. The worst seems to be over."

"You should be more careful with wild mushrooms in the future. Perhaps you should stop experimenting, or else learn more."

"How did you know?" he asked, not meeting her eyes as he gazed sheepishly at his own feet.

"I recognized the symptoms, and Mother Dilys kept good records. It seems you have a history of eating the wrong mushrooms."

"There was one I liked once, but I haven't found it again, and I keep trying."

"Why didn't you tell me you'd eaten mushrooms you'd found in the wild? That would have helped me know better how to treat you."

He had the good grace to look ashamed. "I should have known better, and I didn't want you to think I was foolish."

"I have some experience with mushrooms. I can go hunting with you sometime and help you spot the ones that are safe to eat." He got a glint in his eye, and she hurried to add, "Bring Nesta. Then she'll know what's safe to cook with, and she can throw out anything else you bring her before you make yourself sick."

"I suppose I should have listened to her when she refused to eat those mushrooms."

"Yes, you should have. Listening to your wife is good advice, in general."

She continued her way around the market, getting some greens and onions and a small piece of bacon that could be used to season the greens. She hadn't had meat in so long that even that much felt like an indulgence. "How are you set for cheese?" Mair asked her when she reached the dairy cart.

"I think we're good, since you let us have what was left from lunch yesterday. You take very good care of me."

"I have it to spare, as there aren't enough people left in the village to use everything. I store a lot of cheese to get us through the winter, but I might as well share what I have with friends. Isn't it tradition for the townspeople to make sure the healer has what she needs?"

"I don't know. I never learned the details of the transactions, only that we never seemed to go without. But I'm not a healer. I sell tea. It's not right for me to be treated as a healer."

"I just overheard your conversation with the miller, and you've sent Bryn to get herbs for the Chicken Lady. That sounds to me like you're being a healer."

"I'm still just selling herbs. They merely happen to be herbs that are helpful."

"I know for a fact that Lucina is finally getting some sleep, thanks to you. Like it or not, you're our village healer now."

Elwyn considered that she had taken possession of the book, so she probably should be considered a healer. It was unlikely that she would have to deal with anything too complicated in a village like this, so she couldn't fail the people too badly, and considering that they'd had no healer at all for a long time, she was probably better than absolutely nothing. Still, she didn't plan to promote her services. She wouldn't turn away anyone in need of help, but she wouldn't put herself out there as a healer.

Although her supply of coins was gradually growing, she was still leery of spending money that she might later need to keep herself alive if she had to leave this place where neighbors kept her fed, but she still stopped by the peddler's cart to see if he had anything she needed. Most of her herbs came from her garden, but there were some more exotic ingredients that could be useful, especially for the teas she sold to drink. This peddler was selling housewares and sharpening knives, so he didn't have anything she needed. After scanning his cart, she gave him a polite smile as she turned away.

He stepped in front of her, blocking her exit with a leer. She didn't want to back away and lose ground to him, but his breath was so foul that standing her ground was intensely unpleasant. "Leaving so quick, miss?" he asked, and his breath brought tears to her eyes.

"I'm fully equipped with housewares," she said, taking a step to move around him.

He moved to block her again. "And I'm fully equipped with other things. I imagine it gets lonely here."

"No, not really. I'm never alone. Now, if you'll excuse me . . ." She tried to leave again, and this time he caught her arm.

"Maybe you should stay and talk to me. I get lonely on the road, and I haven't seen anyone as pretty as you in a long time."

Elwyn found that difficult to believe, since Mair was right there, and she was far prettier than Elwyn. But she also looked like someone who was more than capable of taking care of herself, while Elwyn still looked delicate after her recent troubles. She'd put on some weight but wasn't back to her usual self. However, the appearance was deceiving, since all that walking meant that she was now solid muscle.

She'd just started to wrench her arm out of his grasp when a voice cried out, "Unhand her, you varlet!"

CHAPTER 10

Everyone in the market turned to see Bryn. His eyes
flashed fury, but the small basket he held over his
left arm made him look less than threatening. Elwyn feared
he really would rush at the man, and a fight might reopen
his wound. She took advantage of the distraction to wrench
her arm out of the peddler's grasp and run toward Bryn—
more to stop him from doing something stupid than to
seek his protection. The other people in the market moved
to block the peddler, Bryn's cry having caught their
attention.

Before anyone else could confront the man, the chicken
that perched on top of the Chicken Lady's head squawked
and flew right at the man's face, its clawed feet extended.
He flailed wildly, trying to fend off the chicken. "Get it off
me! Get it off me!" he screamed.

The villagers surrounded the peddler so that there was
no way he could go after Elwyn. Only then did the Chicken
Lady whistle. The bird calmed completely and flew back to
its usual roost on top of her head.

"Leave now," the miller said to the peddler. "You're not

welcome in this village. If you come back, no one will buy your wares."

"I wasn't selling anything, anyway," the peddler said, spitting on the ground and wiping blood off his face. "Good luck finding anyone else to come to this corner of nowhere." He closed up his wagon, jumped onto the seat, and whipped his horse into motion. Elwyn was relieved to see that he left down the end of the lane that didn't pass her cottage. The thought crossed her mind that this hadn't merely been a drunken lout making an unwelcome advance. He could have been the baron's agent in disguise, though she doubted an agent of the baron's would have left so willingly, unless he was going to report her location to the baron. She shook her head, as though shaking the thought away. She couldn't live with that kind of fear. Maybe it was time she moved on.

Mair asked, "Did he hurt you?"

"No, I'm fine," Elwyn said. "It was just rather unsettling. I don't think he was entirely sober."

"Well, we have no need for the likes of him here," the miller said.

"It wasn't really his fault," Sara Smith said. "She was the temptress. She's a strumpet living with a man in her house. Now what will we do without that peddler?"

"I thought he was your competition," Mair said. "You and your husband make pots and pans. I'd think you'd be glad to see him gone."

Sara turned away from her with a huff. Elwyn knew the smith's wife was wrong, but she couldn't help but wonder if she'd said or done anything that the peddler might have misinterpreted. A couple of people in the marketplace gave her looks that made her wonder if Sara's words had landed on fertile ground.

Fighting to ignore Sara, Elwyn took Bryn's arm and brought him over to the Chicken Lady. "Thank you," she said to the woman.

"'Twasn't me. 'Twas the chicken. They can be fierce creatures when they're riled."

"Well, I appreciate the chicken, then." Elwyn took the jar of sage out of the basket Bryn held and said, "This is for the sore throat. Make a strong infusion of this—steep it in hot water for about ten minutes, then let it cool—and gargle with it a few times a day." She handed over that jar, which he had labeled, she noted, and picked up the second one. "Make a tea out of this one. One spoon of the mixture per cup of water, steep about five minutes and drink a couple of cups of this a day. That should keep any illness from developing into a proper cold. Avoid drafts if you can, and get plenty of rest."

"If you'd like us to make a tea for you, we'll have the shop open and serving tea this afternoon," Bryn added.

"I can't leave my chicks for that long. But I thank you. Here, take more eggs." Her basket was fairly full, so Elwyn took a few more. This would be almost as good as having meat.

"Is there anything else you need?" Bryn asked Elwyn softly as they moved away from the Chicken Lady.

She shook her head. "No. I got everything I came for."

"Then let's go home."

She could feel the shakiness in the aftermath of the incident coming on and nodded. "Yes, let's."

He took her elbow and escorted her away from the market. She doubted he could do much to protect her in his condition, but his presence was reassuring and comforting. It felt good to have someone to lean on.

As soon as they were out of earshot of the market, she said, "'Unhand her, you varlet?' What was that?"

She looked at him to see him looking back at her with a sheepish grin. "I don't know. It seemed like the right thing to say at the time. Perhaps it was my knightly instincts coming to the surface."

"I've never heard a knight say anything like that, other than in stories. And what were you planning to do if the chicken hadn't intervened? You weren't armed, and you could have reopened that wound if you'd tried to fight him."

"You used the distraction from my challenge to break away from him," he pointed out. "Then the villagers and the chicken took care of the rest. It worked perfectly without me having to do anything but shout."

It struck her then that he had come to her defense. Even wounded and unarmed, he'd stood up for her, which was a sharp contrast to the last time she'd been in trouble. The villagers had also rallied around her. Even the ones who didn't know her, who hadn't yet needed her aid, had supported her. She blinked back the tears that stung her eyes and swallowed the lump in her throat. Perhaps she had found a home.

But she couldn't count on Bryn remaining a part of it. He was bound to leave once he was fully recovered, either to return to the home he'd finally remembered or to try to recover his lost memories. She couldn't afford to include him in her idea of home. He was a patient, nothing more.

Back in the cottage kitchen, he said, "He probably left bruises on your arm," and went to the shop, coming back with a pot of salve. "Sit, and I'll see to it."

"I can take care of myself."

"You can't see the back of your own upper arm."

She couldn't argue with that. With a sigh, she sat and loosened the drawstring at the neck of her blouse and tugged it from under the strap of her bodice to leave her shoulder and upper arm bare. He bent to peer at her arm. "There are some red marks here. This should prevent it from bruising too badly." He gently smeared salve on the affected area, and she fought not to shiver at his light touch. He was only touching her arm, but she felt it through her whole body. She clamped down on her magical senses so that she wouldn't feel what he was feeling while he touched her. She didn't want to know since she didn't know which would be worse, that he was feeling something that would complicate matters between them or that he was feeling nothing more than friendly affection.

"There," he said. "That should help. It doesn't look like it should be too bad."

She pulled up the neckline of her blouse and retied the drawstring. "Thank you. And now it's your turn. I want to take a look at your wound." She stood and he took the seat she'd vacated. He took off his jacket and his shirt. She unwound the bandage and surveyed the wound. "Looks like it's knitting well. I'd better remove these stitches, but then you'll need to be especially careful for a day or two." She got her kit and used the small scissors to snip away the knots, then pulled the thread out as gently as she could with tweezers. He hissed sharply a couple of times but otherwise was quite stoic about it. She dabbed the spots where the stitches had been and dropped in some tincture before putting on a clean bandage. "I may put a poultice on it tonight, but it looks like it's doing well. The cut wasn't very deep, which helps. Now, you should go to the sitting room and rest while I get lunch ready."

He stood. "No, you go to the sitting room and rest, and

I'll make lunch. You've been looking after me long enough. It's time I returned the favor."

This was awkward. She wasn't sure how Gladys would take having an interloper in her kitchen. "You know how to cook?" she asked skeptically, hoping she could deter him.

"I think I do," he said, frowning in thought. "I know I have ideas of what I could do with the ingredients you got at the market. Maybe I'm a cook or work at an inn, though I'm not sure what a cook would be doing with armor and a sword."

Elwyn couldn't think of a way to protest. Either she let him try or he would want to help her, and she didn't know what to do with the ingredients she'd bought. "Be my guest," she said weakly, hoping Gladys didn't take offense or interfere.

The way he got to work suggested that he did know what he was doing. His brisk, efficient movements were the sort that came from long practice, so that he could do this automatically. He put butter in a pan and put it on a rack over the fire, then cracked eggs into a bowl and whisked them thoroughly before chopping herbs and adding them to the mix. It looked like Gladys was staying out of the way, until the butter began sizzling in the pan, and the pan moved itself away from the fire.

He didn't notice at first, since his back was turned. Elwyn was just about to jump up to make it look like she was the one who'd moved the pan when he turned around and saw the pan shifting on its own. He glanced at Elwyn, then back at the pan, a crease forming between his brows. "Did that just . . .?" he asked, shaking his head. "No, it did."

"I, um, have some help with the housework," she said. "Helpers often come with healers' cottages. It's a way of freeing us up to look after others without having all the work of taking care of ourselves." She gestured toward the pan that was being shaken over the fire to distribute the melted butter around it. "Meet Gladys. She's been doing all the cooking."

"Nice to meet you, Gladys," he said. "I've been enjoying your excellent cooking." With a wink, he added to Elwyn, "And there you were, taking credit for it all."

"I was trying to hide her from you, since I never know how people will react to magic."

He frowned in thought. "I don't think I have a problem with magic. At least, this news doesn't unsettle me."

It turned out that he was an excellent cook. Elwyn didn't dare say so, but he was better than Gladys. She made good, simple food, but he had a deft touch that elevated food to an art form, and it seemed to be something he enjoyed doing. After the meal, Gladys whisked the dishes to the sink and fluttered the curtains, making it clear she was reclaiming her territory.

Instead of going to the sitting room, they went out to the garden. Elwyn wanted to check some of her plants, but she also wanted to talk without Gladys listening in. "You might be a cook," she said once they were outside. "That was the best meal I've had in ages, since I was at court."

"I wonder if I do that as a trade or if I have a family to look after. Maybe I'm a valet to a nobleman who doesn't have a full household staff. That might explain the armor, if I was traveling with him. But then was he the one who injured me, or was I defending my master, who was then taken by his enemy?" He went silent as they walked around the garden, and Elwyn gave him the space to think, only speaking after a few minutes had passed.

"The fruit trees seem to be coming along," she said when they reached the orchard. "If I'm still here in the fall, I should have plenty of apples and pears, and there will be cherries soon."

"You aren't sure you'll be here in the fall?"

"I can't be sure of anything." After a long pause, she decided she might as well be honest with him. If he was looking for her, he didn't remember that at the moment. "I'm afraid I'm something of a fugitive," she said. "I had to flee my last post, and they were still hunting me down when I found this place. If they catch up to me, I'll have to leave again. I think I want to stay here, but I'm not sure I can. It's been a nice respite, though."

"Why are they looking for you? Does this have anything to do with why you aren't a healer anymore?"

She examined the leaves on a nearby plant before answering, "Something went wrong with a patient. He wasn't that badly hurt, but he died, so I must have missed something. I was accused of deliberately letting him die."

"Did you?"

She bent to smell a rose. Gladys would probably want some petals to make rosewater. "I don't know," she said at last. "I didn't like him. I'd had to rescue many a serving girl from him and deal with the aftereffects. He was like that peddler today, only the court tended to side with him. I have to admit that I wasn't too heartbroken at his death. If I'd stayed where I was, my life would have been easier without him, though I'm sure there would always be someone behaving like he did. I know I didn't deliberately cause his death, but I can't be entirely certain that I did absolutely everything within my power to care for him. I don't think I fought for him the way I might have cared for someone I didn't dislike."

"That's just being human, isn't it?"

"A healer doesn't get to be human in that way. Everyone gets the same treatment."

"You were at a court, not another cottage like this?"

"Yes. For the past five years I was at the court of a duke."

"And that's how you know all about knights."

"A lot of what I did was patch people up after tournaments and training injuries. I did also look after the people within the palace, including the duke's children and the staff, so it wasn't as though I was merely a tournament medic. I was still working as a healer." Eager to deflect the discussion away from her past, she said, "But I'm curious as to how you know so much about my work. It's almost as though you've trained as a healer, and I've never known a male healer."

"I've been wondering that, myself. There are male physicians, and wizards are trained in herbalism." He frowned. "I'm not sure how I know that. I know a great many things that I don't remember learning, but I don't know what I know until I come across it. I'll have to keep trying new things until I get that vital clue that unlocks my memory."

"Perhaps you should see if you've ever worked in a tea shop. I imagine I'll be busy today."

"I was hoping you'd ask."

Elwyn had guessed correctly that people would be coming to the shop after the morning's events in the marketplace, either to check on her or to find out who Bryn was. Bryn was particularly popular in a village made mostly of women. The concentration of women got to be too much for Bryn, as gregarious as he was, and he fled after an hour, leaving the shop to her. She couldn't really blame him. They were all eyeing him as potential husband material, and he had to have felt self-conscious. There was much giggling following his departure.

"Please, ladies," Mair said. "Elwyn already has first claim on him, and after her it's me, so there's no point in hoping."

"I have placed no claim on him," Elwyn said as she refilled teacups. Or had she? It wasn't that she didn't want him. She couldn't want him because she didn't know who he was or whether he was even free. "But I believe it's his choice what he does."

"In which case, the rest of us stand no chance," Hana said with a rare smile. "We saw the way he rushed to your defense in the market."

"Yes, he was almost as bold as the chicken," Mair quipped.

"I'm sure he would have defended anyone in distress," Elwyn said.

"I do hope that peddler doesn't come back," Hana said with a shudder. "I've never liked him."

"His pots aren't even that good," Nesta said.

From there, the conversation drifted to housewares, to Elwyn's relief. When she closed the shop and went to the kitchen that evening, she found Bryn working along with Gladys to make dinner. "I don't think I've worked in a tea shop," Bryn said with a rueful smile. "I'm sorry I abandoned you."

"I was fine," Elwyn said. "And they were glad you were gone so they could discuss you thoroughly."

"Do I want to know what they had to say?"

"That you were almost as bold as the chicken," she said, trying to keep a straight face, but unable to hold back a smile.

"Accurate," he said.

"I did make it clear that it was up to you to choose which woman in the village you want. No one has a claim."

"Do I have to?"

"Of course not. If we're lucky, you may start getting baked goods and other treats delivered as they try to woo you."

"I don't know whether I've been wooed before. I don't think I want to be right now. Do you think you could claim me, in a purely protective move?"

"Most of them assume I already have."

He stirred some herbs into the pot simmering on the stove. "That's good, then."

Maybe it was. But that wasn't likely to end well.

CHAPTER 11

The next day, Gladys finished cleaning out the spare room and had set it up for Bryn, who was now fit enough to climb the stairs. She'd even removed some of the frillier decorative touches and had done what she could to make it look more masculine. Elwyn had to admit that she felt somewhat self-conscious knowing he was just across the landing from her, especially after what Sara Smith had said the day before at the market. Elwyn suspected the villagers would be disappointed to learn that everything was perfectly proper and they had separate rooms.

He continued to heal, and after another couple of days his wound had become a fresh pink line. She was no longer concerned about it reopening or festering. "So, I'm healed?" he said as he put his shirt back on after her exam.

"You might want to keep it bandaged while that skin is new, so it doesn't get chafed, and I would suggest returning to your normal activities gradually. Don't overdo it."

"If only I knew what my normal activities were."

"Nothing's come back to you?"

He shook his head. "I do get the occasional flash that

feels like it might be a memory, but before I can grab on to it and consider it, it disappears. It's like trying to capture mist. Do you have anything you could give me that could help spur memories?"

"Every preparation I have that's supposed to help the mind is more about moving on from the past and putting memories behind you. I don't have anything that brings back lost memories. Rosemary is supposed to make you more alert and sharpen your memory, but it doesn't have anything to do with bringing back your entire past."

"If it was an injury, it should have healed by now, shouldn't it?"

"If it had been a head injury, you would have had more headaches and dizziness in the first place. You never did, did you?"

"No. But what else could have caused it? Magic?"

She hesitated before saying, "That's a possibility. Your unconsciousness when you first arrived seems to have been largely caused by magic."

"It was?"

"It responded to a potion I have that counters the effect of magic. It wouldn't have broken a spell meant to make you unconscious, but if the unconsciousness was a side effect of another spell, it would wake you, and it did. But it didn't restore your memory."

"Which means it was a memory spell?"

"Maybe. My knowledge of magic is extremely limited. I know only enough for healing and to have some potions to counter magical injuries."

"Why didn't you tell me sooner?" He didn't sound angry, merely curious.

"I was worried about affecting your memory. If I told you too much, you might have developed false memories based on that knowledge, and then you later wouldn't have known what was real. But as long as this has gone on, I might as well tell you now. I'm not sure anything will affect you at this point."

Later that morning, she looked out the kitchen window to see him swinging the sword as though he was fighting. He looked like a little boy playing at being a knight, but unless the spell blocking his memory had also blocked his knowledge of swordsmanship in a way it hadn't blocked his memories of herbs and cooking, she doubted he'd ever been a knight. She went out to the garden and barely held back her laughter. "What?" he asked, noticing her presence and her smile.

"Is that what you think knights do?"

"I was exercising. Rebuilding my strength." His waves of the sword became much more regular, straight up and down and from side to side rather than lunging at an invisible opponent.

She came around behind him, caught his arm, and guided it through the major positions for fencing. That brought back the memory of the duke doing the same thing with her as he helped her to understand what the knights did so she could better see to their injuries and make sure they were able to fight again. "Like this," she coached. "Don't swing so widely. You want to keep your sword so that it defends your body. When you swing so far to the side or up or down, it leaves you open for your opponent to strike."

"Which may be how I got that wound. I let my opponent reach me."

"Possibly. Your wound in the gap between the breastplate and pauldron that shows when you raise your arm too much, and since your armor didn't fit properly, it left a bigger gap than it should have. You also should have had something under the armor to protect that gap, such as mail or a padded doublet."

He turned around within her grasp so that he was facing her, his eyes bright blue in the sunshine and directly in front of her gaze. That also reminded her of the fencing lesson with the duke and what it had led to, and she quickly released him and stepped backward. "So perhaps I had a sword I didn't know how to use when I needed it to defend myself," he said, seemingly oblivious to the way he'd affected her. "But I still wonder what I was doing wearing armor that didn't fit and with a sword I didn't know how to use, apparently fighting someone who also had a sword."

"If we knew that, it would solve a lot of mysteries about you."

"I was hoping using the sword would bring something back, but if I'd ever known how to use a sword, that seems to have gone with my other memories." He took a step closer to her, closing the distance she'd opened. "I am curious how you know so much. You said you treated fighters after tournaments, but how did you learn how to use a sword?"

"When I was working at the duke's court, I observed the knights in training. The duke even taught me a little so I'd better understand how knights might get hurt and what they needed to be able to do when they recovered, but I'm no fighter."

"You've known all along that I was never really a knight, haven't you?"

"I don't know anything. I merely guessed. You weren't wearing the right gear under the armor, and you didn't have the physique of the knights I've known."

"And you didn't tell me this because you didn't want to influence my memory?"

"Exactly." She winced and added, "I'm sorry."

"No, it's actually something of a relief. If I were a knight, it seems like I'd have been a terrible one."

"But you do seem to have the heart of a knight," she said, reaching out to him and giving his arm a squeeze.

"Well, that's the important part, isn't it?" he said with a grin.

"Now that I think about it, it's not much of a compliment, considering some of the knights I've known. All that stuff about honor is mostly in books and songs. The real ones can often be unpleasant. What you know is far more valuable."

"I did valiantly come to your rescue."

"That you did."

"Though not quite as valiantly as the chicken."

"I'm not sure how much of that was valor and how much was meanness."

"It was well-targeted meanness that was a little uncanny, if you ask me. How much do you know about the Chicken Lady?"

"Not much. No one even seems to know her name. She's not mentioned in the healer's log book, so she must be fairly healthy. She's generous with the eggs, and she always has at least one chicken on or around her."

"This village is full of mysteries. And now I'm one of them. So we know I'm probably not a knight, in spite of being armed, I'm literate, I know herbs, and I know how to cook. The valet theory is the best we've got. Maybe we were attacked and my master was captured. Have we heard anything about missing noblemen?"

"I've had no news from the outside world. We'll have to

ask the next peddlers who come through, if our friend from the other day doesn't tell them all to avoid us."

"I would imagine they'd be more inclined to see that this gives them an opportunity with less competition. Of course, I don't know what I know about peddlers, but are they that organized?"

"I have no idea. I just hope one selling tea comes soon because I'm almost out. Speaking of which, it's time to open. Since you're almost as brave as a chicken, are you willing to give helping me another try?"

"That certainly does take valor, but for you, dear lady, I am willing." He gave her a courtly bow.

"I thought we decided you aren't a knight, so you don't have to act that way."

"I rather enjoy it."

Soon after they opened, Mair came running into the shop. "We're going to have a festival!"

"When? How?" Elwyn asked.

"Tomorrow night. Some traveling musicians came through town. They're staying in one of the empty cottages and they said they'd play in exchange for the rooms and food."

"That's rather short notice, isn't it?" Bryn said.

"What planning is there to do? We have musicians. People can bring food. Old Royden has already said he's got a sheep he was planning to slaughter, so there will be a roast. We'll put up a few lanterns to make it look festive. You have to come." To Bryn, she added, "Especially you. We need men. Do you know how to dance?"

"I have no idea."

"No idea how to dance, or no idea whether you know how to dance?"

"Let's just say I don't remember dancing."

"Maybe it'll come back to you. Or you could learn. You're clever."

"I'd be better at the cooking, if they need help with the roast. Could they open the kitchen at the inn? I'd imagine they have the right kind of hearth for that."

"He can cook?" Mair asked Elwyn.

"He can. Though I don't know what he can do with a roast, as we haven't had much meat."

"Well, then, you're up for helping with the roast. I hope I can also count on you to help set up. Can you offer some flowers, Wyn?"

"Of course."

"Then it sounds like we're set." With a wink at Bryn, she added, "Save me a dance," before running off, presumably to make more arrangements.

"It will be good for the village to get together," Elwyn said, as though she was trying to convince herself. "Though I must admit I'm surprised that traveling musicians would come through here." She couldn't help but wonder if they were here for some other reason.

"Maybe they were drawn here the way everyone else seems to have been."

"I don't know what they'd do here if they stayed unless they have skills beyond music."

"Do you know how to dance?"

"It depends on the kind of dance. I think I remember some of the country dances from when I was younger, and I occasionally danced at court."

He held out a hand to her. "Let's see if I remember anything."

"We'd need music. And most of the dances require other people. There's a whole pattern involving circles, squares, or rows of people."

"Well, what do individual people do? If we were dancing together, what might it look like?"

"We'd face each other and bow to each other." He bowed at the waist, and she curtsied in response. "Then in most of the dances we'd step forward and back, then we might turn around each other and return to our places." They did that, with him taking her hand to spin her when they turned around each other. "It looks like you do remember this," she said.

"No, not at all. I just thought that would be fun. What next?"

"That depends on the dance. You might move down the row and change partners, or you might work in a pattern with the people next to you. There's usually someone who calls the dances, telling you what to do next. I wonder if there's anyone in the village who can call a dance. Or maybe the musicians can."

"What's the difference between the country dances and the courtly dances?"

"The country dances tend to be more boisterous. At court, you glide and try not to look like you're enjoying yourself too much."

"I suspect I've never danced. Nothing about it is familiar. I don't seem like a such a serious person that I'd never allow myself to have fun, so you'd think I'd have danced a time or two."

"You might be a very important and busy person who doesn't have time for dancing."

"I hope not. That would be a sad life."

A customer arrived, and they had to quit dancing to make tea. Bryn had a talent for selling the baked goods. He could usually convince a person that they absolutely had to have a cake with their tea, though Elwyn noticed that he stopped making sales pitches when they were down to only a couple left. She wasn't sure what she'd do without him if he ever remembered who he was and went home. She was good at selecting the right tea for a person, but he was the one who had the knack for dealing with people and making them feel welcome. They made a lot more money when he was in the shop, and she suspected that a number of their female customers came to see him. She still hadn't decided whether he was truly handsome, but he was definitely attractive when he smiled, and he had a way of making every woman feel special, her included.

That evening after dinner, they took their cakes—the two he didn't sell—and some spiced tea to chairs they'd set out in the garden near the brook, where they could hear the burble of water flowing over stones near the bridge.

"If we cleared out some of the plants, we could put some tables out here overlooking the water," he said. "During the summer, this will be a nice place to sit outside in the shade. Customers might come here just for that."

"I don't know if we have more tables. I'll have to see what Gladys can find." With a smile, she added, "Have you considered that you might have run a tea shop? You seem to be full of ideas for how to sell tea and make the shop more pleasant."

"I thought when I fled in terror the first day that we'd decided I hadn't worked in a tea shop. And why would someone who runs a tea shop be wearing armor, carrying a sword, and getting into a fight?"

She sighed. "I don't know."

"You've never done this, and you also know what you're doing. You really have a talent for selecting just the right tea, the thing the person is craving at that moment, whether or not they know it. How do you do that?"

She might have confessed to some of the magic in her life, but she wasn't ready to tell him about her talent, especially since she tried not to use it for its true purpose but was using it to select tea. That seemed so frivolous. It wasn't as though she was refusing to use it to heal, though. She'd used it to help him, and beyond that it hadn't come up. She'd yet to have a patient she couldn't help without reading them.

"It's the power of suggestion. If you tell someone you've chosen something just for them, they'll think it's exactly what they wanted."

"Clever!"

They sat in silence, listening to the babbling brook, nightingales in the distance, and other sounds of a late spring evening. "I do like it here," he said.

"It's a nice place," she agreed.

"I've got to wonder why it's been practically abandoned. Don't you think that's odd?"

"Very odd. There's a secret here. I don't think anyone is hiding anything. I'm not sure they know."

"It's magic, I'm almost certain."

"It doesn't feel cursed. Things grow well. Animals are healthy. The people's needs are met."

"Maybe the people here now aren't the ones who were cursed."

"Do you really think that someone would have cast a curse that didn't affect the smith's wife?"

"Could she be the one who cast it?"

"I doubt it. Apparently, the reason she doesn't like me is that my presence means things can't go back to the way they were. She wouldn't have changed the village with a curse, unless it was a curse that went horribly wrong. I also doubt there would have been a curse that didn't affect the miller."

"He's not that bad," he said with a laugh.

"No, he's not," she admitted. "I think he's trying very hard to be what he thinks of as charming. Alas, he's terribly wrong."

"What would you think of as charming?"

She could have answered that quite simply by saying, "You," but she didn't. "Kindness. Humor. Actually caring what the other person wants and what's good for them. Someone who makes you feel seen. And not feeling like you have to be on your guard when you're around them."

"That's a tall order. Who could possibly live up to that?"

"It doesn't seem like it should be too hard."

"Well, since I'm trying to be charming, should we try more dancing?"

"Out here?"

"Who would see us? Don't tell me you've never kicked up your heels outside."

"And you have?"

"I have no idea. Probably not, but I bet you had a lot of fun before you went to court."

She had that feeling of him seeing through her again, like he was seeing the wild child she'd been. She stood and smoothed her skirt. "Very well. Let's see, some music." She began humming one of the old folk songs she recalled, not from the dances the country gentry held, but from the wild summer she'd spent with Mother Alis after she left home, when she'd danced around a bonfire with a handsome young farmhand whose presence would have given her mother a fit of the vapors. While she hummed, she demonstrated the steps of the dance. He was no dancer, and his clumsy attempts kept making her laugh so that she stopped humming. Soon, both of them were laughing and had given up on dancing.

"I knew you had a laugh in there," he teased.

"Why wouldn't I?"

"I don't think I've ever heard you laugh out loud. You might smile, possibly chuckle, but it's as though you're afraid of letting anyone know you're having too much fun."

"I haven't had a lot to laugh about in a long time."

He gave a mocking bow. "Then I am happy to be of service."

The sky turned red, then purple, and since they didn't have a lantern or candle with them, they knew they had to head inside before it got completely dark. Gladys had lit a lamp for them inside, so they could get up the stairs. They stopped at the upstairs landing to say goodnight. Bryn leaned toward Elwyn, and her pulse sped up in anticipation.

But at the last second, he pulled back. "No, I'm sorry," he said, shaking his head. "It's not right when I don't know who I am or what ties I might have. You might not even like the real me. But know this, the person I am now does like you and could happily stay here with you."

She was still too stunned to speak when he went into his room and shut the door. Eventually, she was able to force her body to move and go to her room. She hadn't been thinking that way about him, but she realized she'd been feeling it. Was it him, or was she merely lonely and he was kind? It was so hard to tell, and whatever she thought or felt about him now, it might not even be real, since he wasn't himself. Or he was more himself than he'd ever been, but wasn't the person he was when his life, choices, and experiences affected him.

All in all, it gave her a lot to think about, so much that

she felt she'd barely fallen asleep when Gladys woke her by pulling the covers abruptly away from her and her pillow out from under her. The first faint light of dawn showed in the eastern window, and she heard Mair crying out from downstairs, "Wyn! I need your help!"

CHAPTER 12

E lwyn didn't have a dressing gown, so she threw her loosest dress on over her nightgown and ran down the stairs. "You can help animals, can't you?" Mair blurted as soon as Elwyn opened the back door. Mair was dressed for milking, with a heavy apron over her clothes and her hair tied back in a kerchief.

"What is it?" Elwyn asked.

"One of my cows seems to be in pain, but I can't tell what's wrong with her. She barely lets me near her, and she just bellows."

"I don't specialize in animals, but let me get some things and I'll look at her," Elwyn said. "Come in and have a seat in the kitchen." She ran up the stairs, meeting Bryn halfway. He wore breeches and a shirt, loose and untucked, and his hair was mussed from sleep.

"What's wrong?" he asked.

"Mair has a problem with a cow she needs me to look at."

He turned and went back up the stairs, since they were too narrow for them to pass, even if they wanted to get that close to each other. She didn't bother dressing fully, just pulled on wool socks and her boots and threw a shawl over her shoulders. When she came out of her room, Bryn was coming out of his room with his boots and jacket on. "I'll come with you," he said.

She got some supplies from the shop. Without more information to go on, she had no idea what she might need, so she brought treatments for the most likely things to have gone wrong. It had been nearly a decade since she'd worked regularly with cattle, but she did occasionally tend to horses around the duke's palace, so she wasn't entirely unfamiliar with large animals. Working with animals wasn't too different from dealing with infants or unconscious people, as they couldn't say where they were hurting or how they felt. The healer had to read them.

Mair led them over the bridge to the dairy, where the cows had been brought to the barn for milking, but one of them bellowed, stomped, and shook her head, so that all the others stayed well away. "Can you get close to hold her still?" Elwyn asked.

"I'll try." Mair handed her lantern to Bryn and signaled to one of her dogs, who herded the cow to the edge of the barn, where she couldn't escape. Mair then slowly approached the cow's head, talking softly and gently until she could catch the cow's belled collar. The cow bellowed, pain filling her cry, and shook her head, but Mair held on. "I don't know how much longer I can hold her," Mair said.

Elwyn took a few deep breaths before handing her basket over to Bryn. She stayed close to the head, where Mair held her, and eased nearer until she could get a hand on the cow's neck. Closing her eyes, she reached out to connect with the cow's feelings. The source of the pain was immediately apparent. The left rear leg hurt. Elwyn sent calming feelings to the cow. That didn't always work, but the cow was receptive and went calmer and more still. "There you go," she said softly. "Now, let me take a look at you. Can I get some light?"

Bryn brought the lantern over and stood behind Elwyn's shoulder as Elwyn ran her hands over the cow, making a show of having to look for the problem. She was sure the others knew what a healer could do, but she wasn't entirely comfortable with being too obvious about it. Her examination was far too cursory if she hadn't already known where the problem was. It wasn't all just for show, though. Her touch on areas that didn't hurt helped her build trust with the cow so she'd have a better chance at examining the area that did hurt.

She reached the affected leg and ran her hands down it. The flesh was warm, but unbroken. The cow fidgeted under her touch, but she sent more calm to her and examined the leg more thoroughly, giving it another scan. "It's the leg," she said. "Looks like a strain or sprain. She must have twisted it, but the bone appears to be intact."

"What do you need?" Bryn asked.

"The liniment."

He set down the basket of supplies and held the lantern over it so he could search through the bottles. He handed her one, then held the lantern so she could see to work as she rubbed the liniment into the injured leg. It contained herbs that would help heal the strained muscles and ease the pain. The cow relaxed visibly as Elwyn worked. "Now I'll need some hot water to make a poultice."

"There's a kettle on the fire," Mair said.

"I'll go," Bryn said, handing Mair the lantern. Mair pointed him toward the house.

"He seems to be useful in a crisis," Mair said as soon as

he was gone. Elwyn knew Mair was feeling better if she was teasing her.

"He's useful in a lot of ways," Elwyn replied, then hurried to add, "But not like that." She didn't have to look at Mair to know she was grinning. Elwyn couldn't help but remember the way he'd leaned toward her the night before, but shoved the feeling aside. "He's a good cook and a better scribe than I am."

"So you've decided to keep him."

"That's not my decision. It's up to him. And there may be someone waiting for him."

"But you want him to stay."

"I don't know."

He returned with the kettle, cutting off their conversation, much to Elwyn's relief. He held the lantern while she mixed herbs, added hot water to make a paste, smeared it on a strip of linen, and wound it around the affected leg. She placed her hand on the cow and did another scan to check for any other injuries, but she felt no pain outside the leg, and even that had eased. "She should be fine in a few days," she said. "You might not want to let her out in the pasture so she can rest that leg. I'll refresh the poultice later."

"Thank you so much," Mair said. She released the cow's collar, and the animal remained still and quiet. "She's my best milker—the mother of that problem child calf—but she does seem to be prone to stepping in holes and tripping over things. I'm afraid she was bred for producing milk, not for brains." She walked with them out of the barn, then said, "Wait one moment." She ran off to the dairy, returning with a jug and a small bundle. "Some milk, cheese, and butter for your troubles. And now I need to get on with the milking. Of all days for this to happen, when I needed an early start. You'll be over to help with the festival later?"

"Of course," Bryn said. "You may be getting a late start, but we're up bright and early."

"There's no market today because of the festival, so as soon as you want to get to the square, we'll have work for you."

The sun was truly starting to rise as they made their way back to the cottage. "I didn't realize you worked on animals, too," Bryn remarked.

"It's not my specialty, but it comes up. Some of the larger farming communities may have animal healers. Otherwise, healers make do. I did my initial training in the country, so I've done a bit. It's been a long time, though."

"You were good with that cow. Me, I wouldn't have gone that close to her. You notice I kept you between me and her."

"I think even that chicken would know to keep clear of a distressed animal with hooves." She was relieved that they'd fallen into their usual friendly banter. She couldn't tell if he felt any awkwardness after what he'd said the night before. For her, there was a constant awareness of him, as though she could feel his presence, wherever he was, and that awareness made her skin sing and her breath catch in her throat. She didn't know if she could go on like this, but she also didn't want it to end.

Gladys had porridge ready for them when they reached the cottage. It was about the time they usually rose, so the day progressed like it normally would have, only with less sleep—and even less than that for Elwyn, since her night had been so unsettled. The shadows under Bryn's eyes suggested he'd had a similarly sleepless night—over her, or was it his worries about his true identity?

They didn't talk about what had happened the night before. Not that there was much they could say. There was no real resolution to the dilemma. Until he knew who he was, they couldn't move forward. He finished eating and said, "I'd better get down to the marketplace and help set up."

"Don't overdo it," she warned. "You may not be back to full strength for heavy lifting."

"I don't know what my full strength is, but I will be careful, don't worry."

"I'll go after lunch. I need to cut some flowers this morning."

"I'll be back for lunch. I'll see you then." He paused awkwardly, as though pondering whether he should make some sort of farewell gesture, then settled for giving her a faint smile before leaving.

She sighed once he was gone. She would be lonely when he left for good. If he left. At the moment, there was nowhere for him to go, but if he ever regained his memories, he likely would leave. Selfishly, she wanted to tell him he should just forget his past and stay. She liked him the way he was and didn't care who or what he'd been. At the same time, he deserved to know who he was and what he'd left behind. What if he had a family waiting for him at home, wondering where he was and why he'd abandoned them? She could only imagine what they might be going through.

No, he'd been right to avoid the kiss and whatever else might have followed it. It wouldn't have been right, and it could have led to a lot of pain.

That meant she had to find a way to help him recover his identity. "Do you have any ideas about how to restore his memories?" she asked Gladys. "I don't think any of your essences will help if it's magic, and my potion didn't do any good. Maybe he doesn't want to remember, deep down inside, and his own mind is protecting him from something. In that case, we probably shouldn't force the issue. Still, I think he needs to know or he'll never be able to move on."

The helper didn't bring anything in from the shop or pantry, so she assumed they didn't have anything in the house. "I wonder if it was magic," she mused aloud. "If it was a memory spell, then my potion wouldn't have negated it." When she finished eating breakfast, she went upstairs to consult her books. Magic was beyond her area of expertise, but maybe one of her mentors had encountered something like this. She didn't find anything useful, but she'd only grabbed a couple of her personal journals with notes from her training. She didn't have her whole library.

What she needed was a wizard, but for one of those she'd have to go to a city, and she didn't dare. The baron would find her immediately. She should send Bryn, she decided, since he was the one who needed help. He was well enough to travel. She had money to give him for the journey. Depending on what he learned, he could either return to his life or return to her. It would be his choice.

He'd more than earned a share of the income from the shop, between his handiwork with the labels, the customers who came mostly to see him, and his knack for selling extra baked goods. She tried to think of how long she'd been on the road before she came to this village. It was hard to tell how long a journey it would be, since she'd taken a circuitous route and had avoided towns, but she thought he might be able to reach a city big enough to have a wizard within a few days.

She counted out the coins he'd need for that many

nights in inns, as well as meals, and then doubled that to cover the return trip. She added a few more coins to pay the wizard. He could travel with the musicians when they left after the festival or he could get a ride with the next peddler to come through town if he didn't want to leave immediately. The one danger was that the person who'd wounded him would know him, while he wouldn't recognize his enemy, but the enemy had to have known where he'd likely be and hadn't come for him, so maybe the enemy was no longer a threat.

That plan settled, she put the purse on the kitchen table and went out to the garden. There were plenty of flowers blooming, and she cut enough to make garlands for the festival. She was sitting at the kitchen table, twining flower stems together in chains, when he returned to the house at lunchtime. Seeing him, she felt as flustered as she had as a girl when the handsome hired hand at a nearby farm looked her way. She felt her cheeks grow warm, and she could barely make herself look at him. She dropped the garland she was making and he bent to pick it up for her.

"Thank you," she said. "How is it going?"

"There wasn't too much to do other than set up some boards on old barrels to make tables. That's done. After lunch, I'll start the roast. The fire's already going in the inn's kitchen, so it should be ready to cook by then. That kitchen is nice. There's a whole fireplace just for roasting, complete with spit. I wonder who I can get to turn the spit. Maybe we'll have to take turns."

They continued discussing the festival over lunch, but she barely took in anything he said, she was so focused on her plan. This was probably the wrong time to bring it up, but she wanted to say what she needed to say before she lost her courage. When he started to shove his chair back after he finished eating, she forced herself to look directly at him and blurted, "I've been thinking, and you need more help than I can give you in order to get your memory back. You need a wizard. You should go to where you can find one. Maybe you could travel with the musicians when they leave. And then if you have someone you need to go back to, you can go to them. If not, you can come back here."

She thrust the purse full of coins toward him. "Here, you've more than earned this with all your help in the shop. I'm not sure I'd have had it at all without you. There should be enough to pay for inns and food on the journey and pay the wizard. You can also take some herbs, since wizards need those."

He took the purse and looked at it like she'd handed him a particularly warty toad. "You want me to leave?"

"No, I don't. But I do want you to be able to move on with your life. What you said last night was true, that it's not right to do anything while we don't know who you are. If you do have someone in your life, they must be terribly worried about you. You should go to someone who can help you. I can't. I don't have that ability. I've done everything I can for you, and this is beyond me."

"I can't take your money."

"Like I said, you earned it. I can earn more. There's enough for you to make the journey back. And if you don't come back, send a message to let me know."

"What if you don't like who I really am?"

"I can't imagine that you'd be all that different. This must be your true self. You might be affected by things you've been through that aren't affecting you now, but I would hope that having lived as the person you are now, you could find that again. You've been reminded who you really are, regardless of who you've been. And like you said last night, I can't be with you now. I want to give us a chance, or else know that it's impossible"

"You're putting a lot of trust in me."

"Why shouldn't I?"

"I don't know, since I don't know who I am. I may turn out to be a total louse who'll take your money and run."

"I'd rather learn that than get involved with someone who turned out to be a total louse, which I find highly unlikely."

"And what about my enemy, the one who gave me this?" He gestured toward where the wound had been. "He'll know me, but I won't know him."

"He hasn't come looking for you, and I should think it would be fairly obvious where you went."

"Unless he left me for dead."

She couldn't help but grin. "In which case, you'll give him the shock of his life."

He grinned in response, and she felt the tension in the room ease. "That might give me a moment's advantage. I'll know if someone looks like they've seen a ghost that this is my enemy." He took her hand and clasped it. "I thank you for your generosity and trust. You're right, we can never move forward until we know, and it's not right for me to remain forever in this state of not knowing. Now, I have a roast to get started so it will be ready in time."

"And I need to help Mair decorate, so I'll join you."

He took the purse up to his room, and she gathered the things she needed for decorating. He helped her carry the baskets of flowers to the marketplace, where the transformation had already begun. Mair had set up lanterns on posts installed around the square. Elwyn wound garlands of flowers around the posts and on the market pillar. It looked like there would be enough torches and lanterns to

SHANNA SWENDSON

light up the place once the sun went down, which was late at this time of year. Bryn stayed busy in the inn's kitchen, roasting not only the mutton but also some chickens. The aroma wafting out of the inn made Elwyn's mouth water and stomach grumble.

Once everything was set up and the meats had been removed from the spits to rest, Elwyn and Bryn went home to change into their festival finery, after a quick check on Mair's injured cow. Mair had brought over more clothes for Bryn, and Elwyn had the new dress Gladys had made for her, ruffles and all. She left her hair loose, even though she was too old to pretend to be girlish and was certainly was no maiden. It had a slight wave from the braids she'd worn for most of the day, but that probably wouldn't last long. Her only shoes were either cloth indoor slippers or her worn boots. The boots wouldn't be good for dancing, but the cloth slippers wouldn't hold up to the wear. For a moment, she allowed herself to mourn her old life, when she'd had many pairs of shoes for all occasions. The duke had been generous—or he'd wanted to make sure she was presentable in his court.

She met Bryn at the foot of the staircase. Mair's brother's festival clothes were perhaps a bit too large for him, the jacket hanging off his shoulders and the breeches loose. He'd made an attempt to tame his hair, but when he turned his head toward her at her arrival, it fell right back across his forehead and into his eyes. The sight of him made her want to change her plans and tell him not to go, but on the other hand, the sooner he went, the sooner they could be together for real, if that was going to be at all possible.

This could be their last night together, and she wanted to make the most of it.

CHAPTER 13

Bryn gave Elwyn a gallant bow, then held out his arm for her to take. "May I escort you to the festival, my lady?"

She took his arm. "I would be honored." But his escort didn't last long. He needed both hands to pick up the urn of floral tea she'd prepared, and she carried a small basket of medical supplies in case of emergencies and a lantern to light their way home, though they had no need of it now.

It appeared that the entire village had turned out, including people Elwyn didn't recall meeting. Word must have spread to the surrounding countryside. Mair ran up to them when they arrived and dropped a floral garland with ribbons hanging from behind it on Elwyn's head. "Isn't this lovely?" Mair said. "This is just what the village needed. What did you bring?"

"A cold tea that should be refreshing after everyone's been dancing," Elwyn said. "I'm afraid I don't have much else to contribute. I am prepared if people get blisters from dancing or if they eat too much and develop indigestion."

"You also brought a lot of the flowers, so you've

contributed plenty." To Bryn, she said, "You can set that urn down on that table, by the ale keg." When he was gone, she took Elwyn's arm and said softly, "He looks rather nice in those old clothes, though they might need some alteration."

"Yes, he does."

She must have sounded wistful because Mair asked, "What's wrong? Did something happen between you?"

"Nothing can happen between us while he doesn't know who he is."

"Ah, yes, I can see where that might be a problem. You wouldn't want to start a torrid affair, only to learn that he's got a wife and children he has to return to. His memory hasn't budged?"

"Not a bit, and I've done everything I know how to do. That's why he's going to leave to go find more help than I can give him."

"He's leaving?"

"He may travel with the musicians when they go, if they'll take him. He needs to know who he is, and he's well enough to travel. If he doesn't have anything tying him down, he'll come back, and then we'll know."

"And you're afraid he won't come back. I think he will, though. The village draws the people who need to be here, and it wouldn't have drawn him if he had ties elsewhere."

"It may not have drawn him. He seems to have been nearby for some other reason, and then he stumbled upon my cottage."

"We don't know how it works, and I choose to see the miracle. Now, come eat."

Elwyn hadn't seen so much food since she left the duke's court. There, great feasts with many courses had been the norm. The people at court took the feasts for granted, but for these villagers, this was a real treat. With contributions from everyone, there was more variety than most of them were accustomed to. The Chicken Lady carved and served the chickens she'd contributed. "I can't believe you gave us some of your chickens," Elwyn said as the lady placed a slice of breast on her plate.

"These are roosters, and they're mostly useless to me. I only need one. The rest get eaten."

Elwyn also got a thick slice of mutton. She could hardly wait to sit and begin eating. She hadn't had meat, aside from bits of bacon for seasoning soups and beans, in months. There were also greens, bread, and cheese, but she ate the meat first, chewing slowly to savor it. Bryn brought his plate over and joined her at the table. "I don't know if I normally eat like this or not, but I think this may be the best food I've ever had, if I say so myself." In a softer voice, he added, "Don't tell Gladys I said that."

"You do seem to have a talent for a roast. I'm sure Gladys could do as well if she had the resources. She's been making the most of what was left in the cottage, what I've been able to grow since I've been here, and what I can trade for." But Gladys would be back to cooking for one soon, so she wouldn't need as much. The thought put a lump in Elwyn's throat.

While people were still eating, the musicians began playing. They had tuned their instruments properly, Elwyn noted, which was a good sign. There were three of them, a piper, a drummer, and a viol player. They played softly during the meal, providing a musical backdrop to the conversation at the table.

The miller and his wife took the seats on Elwyn's other side—with Nesta between Elwyn and her husband, much to Elwyn's relief. Other regulars from the shop stopped by to chat. Elwyn had barely lived in the village for two months, but she actually felt like she belonged. She wasn't treated like an outsider, the way she had been at court. There, she hadn't had a defined place. She was a confidant of the duke's, and she interacted with others when she tended to them, but she wasn't considered a courtier, so they saw her as beneath them. Even if they'd known the position she'd been born into, they still would have considered her to be on the bottom rung of their society.

Here, no one seemed to care where she'd come from. In the absence of a lord, there was no real village hierarchy. If anyone could be said to rule the village, it was probably Mair, and since she'd accepted Elwyn fully, almost everyone else also did.

The only sour note came from Sara Smith, who glared at her as though she hated the festival and it was all Elwyn's fault. Her husband wasn't quite as dour as she was, but he also wasn't particularly friendly to anyone. He gave the impression of someone who would have preferred not to be there. Sara whispered to people and glanced toward Elwyn, as though accusing her of something. As far as Elwyn could tell, she hadn't swayed anyone, but it wasn't for lack of trying.

Elwyn forced herself to ignore Sara and turned her attention to Bryn. "That may be the best mutton I've ever had," she said.

"It's certainly the best I can remember." His expression clouded briefly. "It's also the only mutton I can remember."

"But you knew exactly how to cook it, so you must have had it before."

"I don't know how I knew that. I just knew. It's very strange. What else do I know how to do that I don't know I know how to do it because it hasn't come up?"

"We should run you through the village and let you try a little of everything."

"I'm not sure I'll have time for that before I have to go."

She fought back the wave of melancholy that struck her at his words and forced a smile. "It might be easier to just get your memories back, and then you'll know without having to try to bake bread or forge horseshoes."

"That might have less potential for disaster," he agreed.

The musicians struck up a livelier tune, and those who'd finished eating got up to begin the dancing. She was relieved that Bryn didn't suggest they join the first dance. She continued eating slowly to delay the inevitable. She wasn't sure why she dreaded dancing with him. Perhaps it was because she looked forward to it too much. A glance at him indicated he was watching carefully, like he was trying to learn the dances from observing. She doubted he'd have much luck with that. The villagers weren't doing any of the usual set patterns that she was accustomed to from country society where she'd grown up or from court. They mostly just swung around and twirled. That meant couples danced closely together, not with the sly meeting and parting of courtly dances.

It reminded her of the way the country people who weren't part of the gentry had celebrated. She'd joined them during the summer she'd spent with Mother Alis at festivals around bonfires, where people had danced with wild abandon. She'd shed the last vestiges of the proper young lady her mother had trained her to be and had opened herself up to the magic within her.

Bryn leaned over to her. "This isn't what you taught me."

"No, it's not. They're making it up as they go, not doing formal dances."

"That seems like more fun to me."

More fun, yes, but easier to lose herself if she didn't have to think about the steps, and that could be dangerous. There had been a time in her life when she'd enjoyed improvising without regard to rules, procedures, and the like, but her years in noble courts had given her an appreciation for guidelines that made it clear what she should do and when. As long as it had been since she left that life, she had a difficult time shaking herself out of that way of thinking.

Bryn leaned closer to her, and she feared and hoped he was going to suggest they dance, but what he said was, "Are there no children in this village, or were they not included in the festival?"

She looked around the market square, frowning, and realized he was right. There were no children. The youngest couldn't have been younger than eighteen. She'd thought the fact that she hadn't been called upon as a midwife was because of the lack of men, but had no children been born in the past couple of decades? "None that I've seen," she replied. "That's probably not something we want to talk about here and now."

He nodded. "Of course. I can see how that might be sensitive."

She suspected families with children had left. They'd need to earn more money to live, and with few customers, most artisans wouldn't be able to support a family. As more people with children left, others would follow, until the only ones remaining were those who had no reason to leave. She wondered if there was more to it than that. She'd need to take another look through the logbook to see how long this trend had persisted. It was yet another mystery about this village.

Bryn jolted her out of her thoughts by taking her hand. "I think I'd like to try dancing. Care to join me?"

This might be her last evening with him, so she couldn't lose the opportunity. She stood and let him lead her to the middle of the square, where he took her hands and spun and twirled her around with much gusto. He wasn't any better as a dancer than he was as a fencer, but he was completely unabashed, dancing for his own enjoyment without a care as to what anyone else thought about him. She tried to emulate him, focusing on her own pleasure and on him and blocking out any spectators from her awareness.

This was the way she'd been in her youth, in the brief time after she left her father's house and before she began working at court. There had been a freedom then. A healer in a village didn't have to live up to anyone's social norms. She didn't have to dance following the steps or worry about whose company she was seen in. Here in Rydding was the first time she'd felt that in more than a decade, and she laughed out loud for the joy of it.

"I knew you had that in you," Bryn said, leaning close to speak to her over the sound of the music.

"What?"

"Laughter."

"I laugh. You heard me last night."

"Not like that. It sounds good. You sound happy."

"I am." And she was, she realized. She allowed herself not to worry about her past catching up with her or what her future held and purely enjoy the moment, dancing with a man she was coming to love in a village that felt like home.

He put his arm around her waist and spun her until she was dizzy. They fell against each other, leaning on each other to keep themselves upright, laughing all the while. She closed her eyes to shut out the world whirling around her. That had the effect of making her more conscious of him, as their bodies clung together, his face pressed into her hair and his arms wrapped around her waist. She should pull away, she knew, but she was afraid she'd fall without his support. Since she couldn't move, she figured she might as well relish the sensations. It might be all she had of him after this night, and she wanted to be able to remember this later.

"I might have overdone it," he said with a chuckle. "Let's add dancer to the list of things I apparently am not."

"You're definitely no dancer," she agreed. "It was fun, though. Isn't that the point? Who cares what it looks like?" She felt steady enough to open her eyes and look up at him. The sun had nearly set, so he was framed against a blue sky swirled with pink clouds, and the remaining light gave him a radiant glow, as though he'd stepped right out of heaven.

And now she was getting fanciful. She didn't think she'd drunk that much ale. Maybe this was still an effect of the dizziness, or possibly it was the glee of dancing with a man affecting her brain. He looked at her as though he was feeling the same thing. He opened his mouth to speak, but before he said anything, there came a cry of, "Help!" from near the dining tables.

CHAPTER 14

Elwyn ran to get her medical basket from under the table, then fought her way through the cluster of people to see the Chicken Lady lying on the ground, clutching her throat. "I need space and light," Elwyn ordered. The people stepped back, and Bryn brought one of the lanterns closer. The woman's lips were already turning a faint bluish shade, so there was no time to lose. Whether or not Elwyn trusted her talent, this was the time to use it, when her patient couldn't speak for herself.

She placed her hand on the woman's throat and opened her senses. There was something in there, blocking her airway. It was sharp on one end, poking and digging in so that her coughing wasn't dislodging it. "I think she's choking on a chicken bone," Elwyn said. "Help me get her upright."

Bryn handed the lantern over to someone else and knelt beside Elwyn. He helped her pull the choking woman upright. Elwyn got behind her and grasped her around the waist, pulling her hands in sharply to force an exhale. She checked again, and the bone was still lodged in place. "It

SHANNA SWENDSON

seems to be stuck," she said. She forced the woman's jaws open and tried to probe, but she couldn't reach the bone with her fingers, and she didn't have the necessary tools in her kit. She had Bryn move the woman so that her head hung downward, then tried forcing her to exhale again. The bone moved slightly, allowing some air to pass, but she still needed to get it out, and the sharp end appeared to have dug itself in.

This time, her senses weren't failing her. She knew exactly what the problem was. She just couldn't seem to do anything about it. None of her skills or magical talents were able to help.

She turned to Bryn to suggest he move the patient into a different position, but he seemed to be lost in thought, his eyes unfocused. She was about to tell him to snap out of it, that she needed his help, when the woman coughed again, and the bone came out. The Chicken Lady gasped a few times, then laughed. The villagers applauded.

Rubbing her neck, the Chicken Lady said, "I always said Demon would be the death of me."

"We were eating a chicken named Demon?" one of the villagers asked.

"No. I ate a rooster named Demon a few days ago. I guess I know why my throat was scratchy all that time." She turned to Elwyn and said, "I didn't need your herbs, after all."

"You've had a chicken bone stuck in your throat for days?" Elwyn said.

"I must have been able to breathe around it before, but it moved to a bad place." She picked up the piece of bone that had fallen to the ground. It was much tinier than it had felt in Elwyn's magical probing. "I'll have to grind this up and add it to the feed so I'll get better eggs."

Elwyn called for someone to bring a cup of the cold tea and made sure the Chicken Lady wasn't coughing up blood before she helped her up and onto a bench. Then she needed something to drink, herself. She sat down heavily on a bench and let out a sigh. Someone put a mug of ale in her hand before she had the chance to ask for it, and then Bryn joined her on the bench. "Thank you for your help," she said to him.

He nodded without speaking. He looked rather stunned. Was he squeamish about medical things? He'd shown no sign of that when she was treating his wound. He'd even watched while she removed the stitches. "Are you alright?" she asked.

"What?" He blinked, as though coming out of a daze. Then he shook his head. "I'm fine. But that was incredible, what you did."

"I didn't really do anything. All that moving her around must have jostled it loose."

"But you knew exactly what the problem was." He lowered his voice to a level at which no one nearby was likely to overhear him, with all the noise of the festival around them. "You have a talent, don't you? You read her somehow."

"Let's discuss this at home," she said, equally softly.

"I don't think anyone here noticed, in case you were worried. I'm not sure they'd care."

"That's not my worry."

He nodded, then grinned, looking more like his usual self once more. "Well, this festival has certainly been memorable. We should get some eggs out of this, I should hope."

"She's been giving me eggs all along. I think I've finally paid her back adequately." She shook her head in dazed disbelief. "I'm still not sure how she managed to inhale a chicken bone and keep it in her throat all this time."

"I'm not sure I want to know. It's probably best not to ask that question." He glanced toward where the dancing had resumed. "Another dance?"

"I'm not sure I'm up to it. You go, though, if you like." She'd barely spoken the words when Mair danced by, grabbed him by the hand, and dragged him away. Elwyn waved to him and smiled as she watched him attempting to dance. He looked even more awkward from afar than he'd looked up close when she was dancing with him. No, he was more awkward now, like he'd become self-conscious. Had he been more comfortable while dancing with her? Now he was downright clumsy. He tripped, barely caught himself, stepped on Mair's foot, jumped back away from her, bumped into someone else, then bumped into Mair when he jumped away from the other person. All the while, he had a growing look of panic on his face. When the song ended, he gave Mair a rueful bow and rushed back to Elwyn. No other ladies tried to claim him as a dance partner, which was a sign of how bad he was when there were so few men.

He looked humiliated enough that she didn't dare tease him. Instead, she yawned and said, "I'm not sure how much more excitement I can take. I may call it a night soon. If you'd like to stay, I'm sure Mair would be glad to let you walk home with her so I can take the lantern, or you could walk me home and come back with the lantern."

"No, I think I'm ready to turn in, as well," he said. "We got such an early start this morning."

"Have you had a chance to talk with the musicians about leaving with them?"

"I may wait for a peddler. They don't have room on

their wagon, so I'd have to walk. There wouldn't be much advantage to traveling with them."

She had to admit that she was a little bit glad that his departure was delayed. "A few more days won't make much difference, and you might even reach your destination more quickly if you wait for someone who travels faster."

"That was my thought. Should we take the urn or leave it?"

"See if any tea is left."

He went to the drink table, checked the urn, and brought it back. "It was empty," he said. She picked up her lantern, used a rush lit from one of the torches to light it, and went to find Mair to say her farewells.

"Leaving so soon?" Mair asked. "The fun has only just begun."

"After that excitement, I don't feel much up for fun."

"Well, thank you for saving the day."

"I didn't do that much. It took care of itself."

"I'm not sure it would have if you hadn't been there."

Elwyn then checked on the Chicken Lady. "How are you feeling?" she asked.

"Perfectly fine. No need to fuss over me."

"You're not spitting up any blood? Any trouble breathing?" It was difficult to find any bare flesh she could casually touch to read the woman, as wrapped up as she was in her shawls. At least she'd left the chickens at home.

"No trouble at all. Now, you're interrupting my eating."

"You know how to find me if you need help," Elwyn said before she joined Bryn to walk home.

Away from the market square, it was much darker. Elwyn wasn't sure there would have been enough light to walk home without the lantern. She was glad they'd left when they did because the event was beginning to catch up with her now that she'd had time to think about it. As soon as they'd passed the last of the village houses and were nearing the bridge, she said, "I did it again. I completely missed something important. When she complained about the sore throat, I didn't even examine her."

"I'm not sure you'd have seen that just from looking in her throat."

"But I have more tools than just my eyes. I do have a gift. Most healers do. It's a kind of empathy. I can feel what a person is feeling, which helps me know where the problem is. That's very helpful if the person can't talk, but even if they can, feeling it tells me things people usually can't describe for themselves. All I had to do was read her, and I'd have known exactly what the problem was, but I didn't do that because I stopped trusting my gift after that other incident." She gave a bitter laugh. "It seems that not using my gift because it failed me meant that I failed again."

"Have you ever considered that you weren't wrong before, that it wasn't your fault?"

"He died, so I had to have missed something."

"Did you get a chance to examine him afterward and see why he died?"

"I confirmed that he was dead. My gift doesn't work on the dead, so I couldn't read him, and I didn't get a chance to do a thorough physical examination."

"So he could have died for some other reason. The knight he'd fought against might have finished the job."

"He had no new wounds. I know that much."

"There are other ways of killing people."

"Murder by poison seems unlikely. Knights may not be as honorable in reality as they are in stories, but I can't imagine another knight murdering a tournament opponent, especially since the knight who died was the one who lost."

"Could he have been killed to strike at his lord?"

"If so, his lord wasn't the one who suffered from his death. His lord accused me." She shuddered at the memory of shouted condemnations, with no one taking her side.

"Would anyone have benefited from getting you out of the way?"

"Most people barely knew I existed. I don't see why it would be worth killing someone in order to falsely accuse me of murder. Unless . . ."

"Unless what?"

"I had grown close to the duke. He trusted me. I didn't advise him, but he talked to me about issues at court, and the like. He said talking to me helped him organize his thoughts. It's possible someone thought there was more to it than that and wanted me out of the way so they could have influence. If he was talking to me, then he wasn't talking to them."

"Could the baron who accused you have felt that way?"

That hadn't occurred to her, and she couldn't believe she'd never considered that the baron had been scheming against her. "He never liked me. I always got the feeling he thought I was turning the duke against him, though I don't recall ever saying anything about him to the duke. The most I ever did was report that knight for his behavior at court. I mostly avoided the baron. It's hard to believe that would be worth killing his own man for."

"But it's still possible that you had nothing to do with the knight's death and your gift was never in question."

It would be nice to think that way, but even if she convinced herself, she wouldn't be able to sway anyone at court. "It would have been impossible to prove otherwise, and they were convinced enough to pursue me across the kingdom. If they'd merely wanted me out of the way and out of the duke's good graces, they had that."

"They might have worried you knew too much and could reveal the plot. You were a loose end that needed tying up."

"I'm still a loose end. They merely haven't managed to find me here yet."

"Maybe they won't. Maybe they won't think to look for you here because they don't know this place exists."

They'd reached the cottage and the door swung open in greeting. "Thank you, Gladys," Elwyn said as they entered and the door closed behind them. "The festival was lovely. I wish you could have seen it."

They went up the stairs, and lamps in their respective rooms lit as they parted on the landing. "Good night, Wyn," Bryn said.

"Good night, and thank you for your help. I don't think we would have saved her without you helping me move her around."

"It was good to feel of service."

She thought that was a strange way of phrasing it, but he was clearly exhausted. Perhaps he wasn't as thoroughly healed as he liked to believe. He still needed rest, and all the activity preparing for the festival plus the dancing may have been too much for him. She knew she barely had the energy to remove her clothes and do a quick wash at the basin before she fell into bed.

He wasn't in the kitchen when she came to breakfast the next morning, and she worried he'd changed his mind and left with the musicians. Surely he would have said goodbye or at the very least left a note. He wouldn't have slipped away before dawn without a word. Even if he didn't want a goodbye scene, he would have left some kind of notice for her so she'd know what had happened to him.

She'd eaten and had gone to the shop to see to a patient with indigestion from the festival before Bryn came inside. "Come look," he said, taking her hand and bringing her out of the house and around to the side that overlooked the brook. A few small tables with chairs set at them had been arranged between the house and the brook. Some of the plants had been cleared away to make room for the tables, but it still felt like sitting out in a garden. "What do you think?" he asked.

"It's lovely! But you didn't have to do all this yourself. I would have helped."

"It wasn't that much. And I wanted to surprise you. We talked about it, and I think your customers will like it."

"Where did you find the tables?"

"Around," he said with a shrug. "There were some in the shed, in the storage part, not the workshop. I also found a few around the village. If anyone moves into some of the abandoned cottages, you may have to give them back."

"Thank you. Even if the customers don't like it, this will make a nice place for us to sit outside." She noticed, though, that he had spoken of 'you' rather than 'us,' and she couldn't help but feel like he was setting things up for her to function in his absence. That made sense, and she reminded herself that him leaving had been her idea. That didn't mean she was happy that he seemed to have embraced the idea and was making preparations.

She wasn't expecting a lot of customers the day after the festival, since she was sure most people would be recovering or cleaning up, but Mair, Hana, and Lucina arrived soon after she opened, eager to rehash the events of the night before. She took them out to the tables by the brook. "See what Bryn set up for me," she said.

"You'll have trouble getting rid of people now," Mair said, taking a seat at one of the tables.

"I won't put out lanterns for after sundown," Elwyn said.

"Speaking of sundown, you two left early last night." Mair winked and grinned.

"After a woman nearly died on me, I wasn't feeling very festive. As I told you last night."

"But you saved her," Lucina said. "You didn't feel like celebrating?"

"I didn't really do anything to save her. I felt so helpless. She was lucky. I'm still wondering how she managed to inhale a chicken bone."

"She must eat very enthusiastically," Mair said.

"She was fortunate you were there," Lucina said. "It is good for this village to have a healer. You have helped me."

"You're sleeping better?" Elwyn asked.

"Yes. I still have the nightmares, but they are not as bad. I took your advice and have been writing them down, and I have realized that most of them are not memories. They are exaggerations of what happened, or they are what I feared might happen but that did not. Thinking about that seems to have made them less frightening, so they don't wake me up as often."

"That's good to hear."

Mair raised her teacup. "Here's to our healer! I haven't had a cold since I started drinking your tea, and Lucina is sleeping better."

"It's nice to know I'm doing some good," Elwyn said, looking down at the table so she wouldn't have to look them in the eyes. She felt like she was hiding from them in not telling them the full story of why she had come to be there. In spite of what Bryn had suggested the night before, she still wasn't sure she trusted herself. It just didn't make sense for the baron to kill his closest ally in order to drive her away from court. It was nice of Bryn to try to make her feel better, but he didn't know what had really happened.

"This village changed for the better when you arrived," Mair said. "Not only are you healing people, but you've given us a place to gather, which has brought us all together, and that then led to the festival."

"That wasn't because of me," Elwyn insisted. "You put together the festival, and it happened because there were musicians in town."

"But I think you were the spark that started it all. Something about having a healer again made us feel like we'd rejoined the rest of the world, like our curse was lifted."

"Curse?" Elwyn asked, curious.

"Figuratively speaking. Whatever it was that made people leave."

"Rydding isn't cursed at all," Lucina said. "It is a safe, happy place, where I have found refuge. Though I wouldn't mind having a few more people to bake for."

"And more men," Mair added. She raised her voice and called out, "Do you hear that, village? Bring us men!"

Elwyn thought perhaps she should have been more specific about what sort of men and why they would come.

CHAPTER 15

The next day, Elwyn approached the market with a mix of dread and hope. She dreaded seeing a peddler Bryn might leave with, but she also hoped one would be there—a trustworthy one with a large wagon and a sturdy horse. She didn't want Bryn to go, but she couldn't stay in this limbo, knowing how they felt about each other but unable to act upon it, much longer.

Ever since she'd given him the money and suggested he go he'd been different, quieter and more serious, as though he had a great deal on his mind. She hoped she hadn't hurt his feelings with her suggestion that he leave. He'd seemed to take it well, and he'd been his usual self at the festival. It was only afterward that he'd seemed different. Had learning about her past changed the way he felt about her? He'd assured her that she wasn't to blame, so she didn't think that was it.

Perhaps he merely needed to think. Making the journey to discover his past was a big decision, and he'd said he was worried about what he'd learn. His distraction might have nothing to do with her.

When she returned and reported that there hadn't been a peddler, he merely shrugged and said, "Maybe tomorrow." He didn't sound too disappointed, but he headed out to the garden without saying anything else, leaving her wondering what she'd said or done. She started to go after him and tell him he didn't have to go if he didn't want to, but she stopped herself. Anything she said would probably only make matters worse.

That evening at dinner, she said, "If a peddler doesn't come soon, I may have to send you to the nearest town with a decent market to buy more supplies. I'll soon be down to mint and chamomile teas until I can harvest and dry the summer flowers. We've used up almost everything that was already dried. I may have to close the shop if I can't restock."

"You really do want to be rid of me, don't you?" he said with a wry smile that contrasted with his sad eyes.

"I said nothing about seeking out a wizard while you're away. It's up to you if you want to track down someone who could get your memories back. I merely need supplies, and I can't go unless I want to be arrested."

"No, it's probably best if you don't go, at least not until you know if you're still the kingdom's most wanted with a bounty on your head." With a deep sigh, he said, "If a peddler doesn't come tomorrow, I'll head out. And I will come back, no matter what, so I can bring you what you need. Make a list for me." He resumed eating, giving the impression that the discussion was over.

"Your outdoor tables are doing well," she said. Conversation between them had gone from easy to difficult, and she didn't understand why, but she kept trying to draw him out. "Though they're part of the reason I'm running out of tea."

"People like sitting by water under a tree. They'll stay all day if you let them. At least, I would."

"Someone paid with a jug of ale today, and it won't last long. Shall we sit outside tonight and enjoy it?"

"How much tea did they drink that it was worth a jug of ale?" He almost sounded like his usual self for a moment.

"It was in exchange for a couple of days of sitting here and drinking tea, plus some to take home, and I gave her a preparation for headaches. To be quite honest, I think the sitting by the brook was the best headache cure."

He stood. "Yes, let's sit outside this evening." With a crooked smile, he added, "I could use a bit of that headache cure, myself."

She jumped out of her seat and moved toward him. "Oh, would you like me to get something for you? Where does it hurt?" Had she missed a head injury, after all?

"I meant the sitting by the brook headache cure. I don't need anything else. It's not even a real headache, just a sort of tension, which drinking ale by the brook should cure."

"If you're sure, but I could check."

"No need," he said, taking a step away from her.

They took a lantern with them and set it nearby, but not on the table, so they sat in near darkness as the sun went down. Elwyn could hear the brook babbling as it flowed over the stones near the bridge. Night birds called out, but other than that, the night was peaceful. "I used to think I liked the bustle of court life, and I thought country life was boring, but I'm enjoying the peace here," she said.

"You were a country girl?"

"I was the oldest daughter of a minor squire in a back-water county. It was a half-hour walk to the nearest village, which was no larger than this one would be if it were fully occupied. The healer's cottage was along a shortcut that went through the woods. She didn't live in the village itself. My mother wanted me to marry above our station so I could help elevate the family, and she preferred that I spend my time in music and dancing lessons and attending balls so I could meet eligible young men. I preferred to wander in the woods, and I often ended up spending my days with Mother Alis, learning about herbs and healing."

"Ah, I thought I detected a bit of wildness to you beneath all that courtly reserve."

"I don't have courtly reserve!"

"Call it serenity, then. Or self-control. But the wildness lurks beneath. You must have been miserable at court, having to watch everything you said and did."

"I think maybe I was. But mostly I was lonely. I didn't realize it at the time. I enjoyed the status and the comfort. It seemed like a better life than living in a cottage in the woods and tending to sheep as often as I treated people."

"How did you come to be a healer? Did you always know what you wanted to do?"

"In a way, I suppose. I loved learning about herbs and how to use them, but I didn't imagine it was a life I could have. Once I discovered the magical talent and learned to use it, I couldn't imagine doing anything else, and I knew it would be wrong to waste the gift."

"But you knew for certain you had the gift, and you were able to use it."

"Yes. Actually, I'd been using it all my life without realizing what I was doing. It was useful for manipulating my parents and my sisters. I knew just how they felt and could persuade them by playing on that. It was when I tried to use it on Mother Alis that she recognized what I was doing and tested me. She realized I was a born healer. Maybe that was why I was so drawn to her cottage. I enjoyed working in her garden far more than I like music lessons."

"I imagine your mother wasn't open to you going off to train to be a healer instead of marrying nobility."

She gave a wry chuckle. "My mother had just managed to get a hideous baronet interested in me. She wasn't going to give up on her dream so that I could live in a cottage and commune with peasants. My parents absolutely insisted I marry, so I ran away from home, and my family disowned me."

"That's why you didn't return to your family when you fled the duke's court?"

"My family home would have been the first place they looked for me, but I wouldn't have been welcome there." She laughed softly to herself. "My mother would have been doubly furious to learn that I'd made it to a duke's court, only to ruin everything and have to flee. Anyway, I spent a year or so training with Mother Alis before she sent me on to another healer in a different village. She didn't think the local people would ever accept me as a healer, having known me all my life and knowing my origins, so I couldn't replace her, and she wanted to start training a replacement. I worked another few years in a village before moving to a town, and from there began getting positions at various courts, first with an earl, then later with a duke. And then all that ended when I had to flee. I was on the run for a few months before I came here. Every time I thought I'd found a safe place, someone recognized me and reported me, and I barely got away. By the time I came here, I was just about starving to death. I had no money, and I didn't dare work as a healer, lest someone realize who I was."

"And you found your way to Rydding."

"Fortunately. Though I did resist healing. I thought the tea shop would be a good compromise."

"You were using your gift, though. That's how you know exactly what kind of tea a person is craving. It's not merely suggestion."

"I do use it for that sometimes," she admitted. "In fact, that's about all I've used it for lately, other than when I treated you and the Chicken Lady. And the cow."

"Because of that incident before?"

"Yes. I couldn't trust that sense anymore."

"You were right with me, with the cow, and with the Chicken Lady. Are you right about choosing the teas people want?"

"No one's complained, but I suspect suggestion does play a role there, as well."

"Has it ever failed you other than that one time with the knight?"

"Not that I'm aware of. I wasn't perfect when I was training, but my mentors were there to back me up then."

"So maybe you are born to do this. Trust yourself. That's the best way you can use your talents and help others. You have a purpose in life. Appreciate that."

She waited for him to say something else, but all she heard was the brook. "I'm sure there's something you're meant to do that you're good at," she said reassuringly after the silence became uncomfortable. "We merely haven't found it yet because it's not something that's done here. You have an excellent hand. You may be a scribe. You might be a schoolmaster or a scholar. Or there's always your idea about being a valet. You are a good cook."

"No, I don't think so," he said, his voice so mournful that it made her heart break.

"This is why it's important for you to get your memories back. You can't go on like this, not knowing where you belong or what you can do. Or else you have to treat this as a blank slate and start over, doing what you want to do, without worrying about what happened before. The only problem there is not knowing if there's someone out there who would be worried about you."

"Yes, there is something about that blank slate, not only not knowing the good things, but also being blissfully ignorant of the bad things from my past."

"Lucina has nightmares about her past. That hasn't plagued you, has it? Have you had nightmares that might be clues?"

"No, I don't think my past has come to me in dreams."

"So that much is good, I guess."

He stood and said, "I'm ready to turn in. I can find my way inside without the lantern if you'd like to stay out longer."

"No, I think I'll join you. Going inside, I mean." She was glad it was too dark for him to see her face flushing. She was far too old to be acting like this about a man.

He picked up the lantern and led the way to the back door. He let her take the lead going up the stairs. She paused at the top and said, "Well, good night. Pleasant dreams."

Much to her surprise, he bent and kissed her on the lips. It wasn't merely a friendly kiss. There was warmth and passion in it, and it started a fire spreading through her. Had he changed his mind about not getting more involved until he knew he wasn't being unfaithful to someone else? She was just starting to recover from the initial shock to return the kiss when he broke it off abruptly. "Good night, Elwyn," he said, entering his room and shutting the door behind himself.

She was in her own room when it struck her that he'd used her real name, which she'd never told him. Had she let it slip or had he guessed? Was she even sure that's what she'd heard? But then she remembered something else from their conversation the night of the festival: She didn't think she'd ever mentioned that the person looking for her was a baron, but he'd referred to the baron who was looking for her.

She sat down hard on the edge of the bed, stunned, as the realization hit her. He must have regained his memories. That was why he'd been in no rush to go find a wizard, why he'd been so different, why he'd kissed her. And if he knew her real name and about the baron, then she'd been right that he was here because he was looking for her.

Grabbing her lantern, she stormed out into the hall and banged on his door. "What did you just say?" she shouted. "You remember who you are, and you know who I am, and I want to know how that connects."

There was no response from inside the room. She tried to open the door, but it had been locked or was blocked. She hadn't even thought there were locks on these doors. "Gladys?" she called out. "You'd better be on my side in this. Help me out."

The door flew open, and she found herself staring at Bryn—or whoever he was—who stood just a few feet behind the door. "You owe me an explanation," she said.

He sighed wearily. "I do. But how did you know?"

"You called me 'Elwyn.' I haven't told you or anyone here my real name. You had to have remembered something, and if you remembered my name, that means you knew about me from before you came here. I also realized that you know the person looking for me is a baron, and I didn't mention that. Are you working for him?"

He closed his eyes in an expression of pain that was stronger than anything he'd shown when she was treating his wounds. "I was. But it's more complicated than that. Can we go to the kitchen to discuss it? I need one of your soothing teas."

Elwyn was somewhat disarmed by his response. She'd been prepared for denial, possibly for his mask to drop completely as he revealed the true villain he was. But he just seemed sad and resigned, possibly ashamed. She hated to agree with him while she was still so angry, but she didn't think this was a good conversation to have in a place as intimate as his bedroom, and she could use some of that soothing tea, herself. "Yes, let's go downstairs," she said, stepping back so he could exit. He may have suggested it, but she didn't fully trust him not to slam the door and stay in his room once she turned to head down the stairs. She supposed he could flee when he went down the stairs ahead of her, but she didn't think Gladys would let him leave the house.

The lanterns in the kitchen had already been lit, and a pot of tea was steeping when they entered the kitchen. Bryn waited for her to sit before he sat on the adjacent side of the table, where he wasn't directly facing her. "How long have you had your memories back?" she asked.

"It happened the night of the festival. When you were working on the Chicken Lady and you couldn't get the bone to dislodge, there was something in me that said I had to act and that I could do something. I was able to make it move out of her throat, and that seems to have broken the spell."

"You used magic?"

He hesitated, gripping the edge of the table until his knuckles turned white, before he said, "It turns out that I'm a wizard, though not a very good one, I'm afraid. I was suffering from my own memory spell, and using magic instinctively seems to have broken my spell."

"Why did you take away your own memories?"

He gave a rueful wince. "I didn't mean to. As I said, I'm not a very good wizard. In fact, I'm still an apprentice because I've never managed to pass any of the exams to be able to leave my apprenticeship. At this point, I'm really just an assistant to my master. There's no teaching anymore, and I've long since passed the end of my official apprenticeship obligation, but without having qualified as a wizard, I can't get any other kind of job."

"That's how you know all about herbs."

"One thing I am good at is making potions. That's most of what I do for my master, aside from essentially being his household servant, which is how I know how to cook. I suppose you could say I'm the Gladys of my master's house. It's my attempts to do spells that tend to go horribly wrong."

"What's your name—your real name?"

"Gareth," he said, wincing again.

"I definitely think you're more of a Bryn."

"My name is about the only thing my parents gave me. They died in a plague outbreak when I was very young, and I was sent to an orphanage, where I caused all kinds of trouble from accidentally using magic, so they sent me for training. Unfortunately, it turned out that training didn't help much for controlling my talents. I didn't do as much damage from accidentally using magic once I was trained, but when I tried to use magic I caused even more mayhem when it went awry. Magical training for me was mostly about learning how not to accidentally use magic. Oh, and I have no wife or children. Not that this likely matters anymore."

Gladys poured mugs of tea and slid them down the table toward them. Bryn—or Gareth?—thanked her, and Elwyn added her own nod of thanks before turning back to Bryn. She couldn't think of him as Gareth. "This doesn't explain how you know about me and the baron."

His expression made him look like she'd kicked him in the gut. He took a long drink of tea before saying, "I'm afraid I'm the one who found you and brought him to you."

CHAPTER 16

E lwyn made herself put her cup down before she could give in to the temptation to throw it at Bryn. "You what?" she shouted, rising from her seat and leaning toward him. She remembered worrying that he'd been looking for her, but she'd ignored her own instincts. All this time, she'd been harboring her enemy, even falling in love with him.

"I didn't know you at the time!" he protested.

"But you worked for him?"

He lowered his gaze, then made a visible effort to meet her eyes. "My master worked for him. Please, let me go back to the beginning and explain."

She wasn't sure she could sit and listen to this calmly, but her chair moved against her legs, forcing her to fall back into it. "Do explain," she said through clenched teeth.

"The baron came to my master, saying he needed help tracking an escaped murderer. He had a scarf that belonged to you. My master did a spell to show where you were. It wasn't precise. It just led to a general area. To narrow in closer, the spell would have to be repeated within that area, so a wizard had to travel with the baron. My master doesn't like to travel, so he sent me. But the baron didn't want to be seen dealing with wizards, so he put armor on me, like I was one of his men."

"And you led him right to me."

"I pointed him in the right direction, but before we got here he turned on me. It seemed that he had no intention of apprehending a suspected murderer and bringing her back for a trial. He was cleaning up loose ends, and one of those loose ends was me. He must have figured we were close enough for him to be able to find you without magic."

"That's how you got hurt."

He nodded. "He attacked me. I had no idea how to fight, so I mostly tried to dodge him." He rubbed absently at the spot on his face that had been bruised. "That came from losing my footing and bumping into my saddle. I could feel myself getting weaker once I was hurt, and so I tried using magic out of desperation. I did a memory spell to make him forget where he was and what he was doing and make him want to turn around and go home. But, as usual, it went wrong and hit me, too, wiping out not only the memory of why I was there, but everything else. I guess I got turned around and headed here instead of heading home."

Elwyn wondered if that had been the village luring him. If he didn't have a real home of his own, the village might have been the next best thing. "I wonder how much of an effect it had on him," she mused aloud. "Did he forget who he was or did he merely forget coming after me and how to find me?"

"I don't know. I also don't know how long the spell on him will last or if it can be broken. It's possible that when it broke on me, it broke for him, as well, since it was the same spell."

"So I have to be prepared for him to come here for me."

"I'm so sorry," he said, his face twisted with pain. "I wish I could say that I jumped to your defense when I learned his plan, and that's how I was wounded, but I was trying to save myself. I didn't know whether or not you were guilty, though I did start to wonder when he attacked me rather than let me be present when he found you."

"How soon could he get here?"

"It took about two days to get here. We got a late start, stopped for the night, then were in the woods around sunset."

"So if the spell on him broke at the same time as it broke for you, he could be here sometime tomorrow. Why didn't you tell me sooner?"

"I should have, I know, though I didn't think about the spell having broken on the baron until now. I'm sorry." He looked at her with eyes so full of remorse that she knew he was being honest.

"I'd better leave in the morning," she said

"I'll go with you." She started to protest, but he hurried to add, "He's not going to be happy with me, either. If you don't want me traveling with you, I'll understand, but we don't have to do this alone."

She studied him for a long time. He was different from the man she'd come to know—sadder, more tired. The life had left his eyes. But when he'd forgotten everything, he had become the person he had the potential to be, and she'd liked that person. "We can leave together," she said. "I don't know how long we'll stay together. It depends on where we want to go. I don't have a destination in mind. I don't know if there's any way I can get beyond his reach, and if I use any of my gifts or knowledge, that only makes me easier to find."

"At least you know something you can do. I can't do the one thing I've been trained to do. I can't work as a wizard without passing that final exam, and even approaching another wizard to take me on as an apprentice would make it possible for my master to find me and hand me over to the baron."

"You think he would?"

He gave a bitter laugh. "I know he would. He'd want me dragged back to him, since I'm still technically his apprentice."

"Have you ever considered that your master didn't want you to pass the final examinations because he'd lose his servant?"

"Oh, I definitely failed."

"Let me guess, he constantly berated you and told you nothing you did was any good. You believed you were a failure because he told you so, constantly. And so, you lost all confidence and failed."

"More or less. But believe me, some of my failures were pretty spectacular. Fire was often involved. I haven't even been allowed to use magic at all for the past two years."

"How can you learn to do magic if you're not allowed to use it? But when you instinctively used magic to save the Chicken Lady, it worked—when you didn't expect it not to."

"Unfortunately, I'll never be assigned a new master by the guild, so I can't know."

"There's got to be a way for you to learn and train, and then you could present yourself for the exams." She couldn't help but smile. "You could always work as a cook."

"I'd have to find someone desperate enough not to care about references. First, though, we've got to survive the current situation." He yawned and said, "If we're going to get an early start, we should probably get some rest." He glanced at her in a way that reminded her of a scolded puppy. "Are you still mad at me?"

"I don't know how I feel. For most of the time I've known you, you had no idea. You weren't lying to me or hiding anything from me. But I am mad that you didn't tell me once you remembered. I could have been well away from here by now."

"Honestly, I didn't want to lose you, and I knew that's what would happen as soon as I told you." He stood up and faced her squarely. She could see the effort that cost him. "I love you, Wyn. I think I have ever since the moment I opened my eyes and saw you there, and it's only grown since then. Being with you has been the first time in my life I've felt like I had a purpose, when I could believe in myself. I wish I hadn't got my memory back. I liked who I was without it much better."

"So did I," Elwyn admitted. "But you have the potential to be that person. That's who you are at heart. You'll have to find that person within yourself again. And I will have to get to know who you are, all of who you really are, to know how I feel about you."

"That's fair," he acknowledged. "But I want you to know that my feelings about you didn't change when I got my memories back. If anything, I think I appreciate you even more. I've never had anyone like you in my life before. I would have been different if I had."

"We're all the sum of our experiences, including the people who have been in our lives. Now, good night. I'm leaving at first light."

She picked up her lantern and went up the stairs, still reeling from everything that had come out during the evening. To think, she'd been harboring a wizard who had nearly led her enemy to her—but who had also sent her enemy away from her.

She knew she needed rest, and this could be her last night in a comfortable bed, but she was too restless to sleep, so it was probably better to pack as much as she could before she went to bed, and then she could sleep a little later in the morning. There wasn't much to pack. She didn't have a lot of clothing, and she hadn't taken most of her other belongings out of her bag. All she had to do was put a spare shift, a blouse or two, a skirt, and a few pairs of stockings in her bag, along with her indoor slippers. She'd use her hairbrush in the morning, and she'd pack up whatever food was in the house, along with some herbs that might be useful.

She sat on the bed and looked around the room. It had been a nice enough place to stay, in spite of all of Gladys's frilly touches. It had felt like home, and she hated to leave. She should have known better than to get too attached. Maybe she should have moved on sooner. She knew now it was dangerous to stay in any one place for very long, since any wizard would be able to track her down. She wondered how far that magic worked. Would she ever be truly out of reach? Maybe Bryn—or Gareth, but she had a hard time thinking of him that way—would know.

Or she could stop running. She wasn't sure how she could resolve this. Maybe she could go to the duke while the baron was looking for her and explain. If Bryn was right about what the baron had done and why, that would surely persuade Maxen. He would be able to stop the baron. She didn't have evidence, though. Would Maxen listen to her if the baron wasn't there, speaking against her?

With the beginnings of a plan, she was finally able to get to sleep, and she woke feeling oddly refreshed. She dressed, putting on the duke's necklace, in case she needed it to gain access to the palace, and went downstairs to find Bryn already in the kitchen, trying to pack up some food, against Gladys's objections. When he put something in his pack, Gladys removed it. "Gladys, we have to leave," he said.

"Yes, Gladys, we have to go," Elwyn said. "But we will come back. We have to deal with this."

Bryn turned to look at her. "We're coming back?"

"I hope so. I was thinking about it, and I can't keep running. If the baron can have a wizard track me, I'll never be able to get away from him. While he's probably on his way here, I plan to go back to the duke and explain everything. If you're with me, you can tell him what you know, what the baron did to you. I'm sure he'll listen if the baron isn't there. And then once everything is resolved, we can come back here. You can deal with your master while we're at court and collect whatever belongings you have there that you want. You can start over for good here."

"That sounds utterly terrifying, but you're right, it's probably better than staying on the run." He resumed packing, and this time Gladys let him. While he did that, she went into the shop and collected some of the things that might be useful on their journey. When she returned to the kitchen, Gladys had breakfast prepared and on the table for them, a hearty meal of eggs and toasted bread. Though they were in a hurry, Elwyn tried to savor every bite, knowing it could be the last hot meal she'd have in a while.

Finally, there was nothing to do but leave. The sky was just turning pink in the east and there was enough light to travel. Unless the baron had camped in the woods nearby, he wouldn't reach the village for hours, at the very earliest. This was their best chance.

She put on her hat, wrapped her shawl around her shoulders, and picked up her pack. Bryn fastened the sword belt around his waist. "I may not know how to use it well, but just having it visible may make people think twice about accosting us," he said when he noticed her eyeing the sword. He picked up his own pack, and they headed out the front door.

But they hadn't made it to the front gate before the smith's wife ran into them at a full tilt. Her hair was in disarray, still in her nighttime braids, which were coming undone, and she wore a nightdress under a shawl. "Oh, good, you're already awake," she said, gasping out the words between labored breaths. "You have to come right away. It's my husband."

Elwyn couldn't help but glance down the lane in the direction she expected the baron to arrive from. She couldn't afford the delay, but she also had a duty. On the other hand, Sara had done everything she could to drive Elwyn away. Should she put herself and Bryn at risk for someone who didn't want her there and doubted her abilities?

"It's urgent," Sara said. "Come now!"

Elwyn stifled a groan. As much as Sara had resisted her presence, Elwyn knew it had to be truly urgent for her to come seeking help in her nightgown at dawn. "What is the problem?" she asked. She probably still had a few hours to get out of the village. She wouldn't be as far along the way as she would have liked, but she was still unlikely to run into the baron, if he was even arriving that day. This was merely the earliest she thought he could arrive.

"My husband's unconscious. He was up early shoeing a horse, and something must have happened."

"That's not the sort of thing one treats with herbs," Elwyn said. "I won't be able to do much for him."

Sara caught her gaze with a glare she couldn't escape from. She wanted to turn away, but she was frozen. "You and I both know that you wouldn't be able to stay in that house if you didn't have the gift. Staying in that house means you're obligated to use that gift to help others, so come see to my husband." She glanced at the packs Elwyn and Bryn carried and gave a derisive sniff. "Or were you planning to sneak away from us?"

"We have an errand in another town and were getting an early start," Bryn said. "We'll be back."

"I need to collect some things," Elwyn said. She turned back to the shop and picked up the bag she kept for emergencies, with all the treatments for burns, broken bones, and bruises, as well as the most serious illnesses.

She and Bryn could barely keep up with Sara as she led them to the forge, which lay halfway up the lane toward the castle, near the mill. A lantern burned in the forge, illuminating the man who lay unconscious on the ground by the anvil. Nearby, a horse stood placidly. "Bring that lantern over here," Elwyn said as she knelt by the smith. A bruise was already forming on his temple, so he must have hit his head, but what had caused the fall, and was the bruise the cause of his unconsciousness or the result?

There was only one way to find out when the patient was unconscious. Elwyn had spent months being afraid of that gift, losing trust in it. But she had used it for the Chicken Lady and Bryn, and even on a more minor level she'd been accurate in selecting the right teas for people. Maybe Bryn was right and someone had killed the knight. Now wasn't the time to doubt herself. She placed her hands on the unconscious man's forehead and opened her senses to feel what he was feeling.

The first thing that struck her wasn't an ache in the head. It was a gripping in her chest, as though someone was squeezing her heart as it beat erratically, fluttering rather than truly beating. That was why he'd fallen. She broke the connection with a gasp and ignored the wife's queries as she dug in her medical bag for the vial she needed. This tincture could be a poison or a cure, and the line between the two was very fine. She'd have to open a connection with him again in order to read the exact moment to stop the dosage. "I need you to hold his mouth open and his tongue up so I can reach the bottom of it," she said to Bryn.

When he had the smith in position, she carefully dripped one drop of the solution onto the underside of the man's tongue. She placed her free hand on his head and opened her senses again. The tightness in the chest had eased, but it was still there. Keeping herself connected, she dripped in another drop. Already, she could breathe more easily, and so did the man, who began to stir. She handed the bottle over to Bryn and went deeper, searching for any other issues. The ache in the head didn't go below the surface. The problem was all with the heart. He would require ongoing care to prevent this sort of occurrence again, but he was now out of immediate danger.

She dabbed salve on the bruise to speed its healing, and as she did so, the man's eyes opened. "What happened?" he muttered.

"Your heart tried to kill you," Elwyn said. "Have you been feeling lightheaded?"

"Sometimes, off and on, when I overdo it. But it gets better if I rest."

Bryn had to pull back Sara when she flew at him. "You've been feeling bad, and you said nothing?" she shrieked.

"I didn't think it was that bad," he muttered, rubbing his chest. "Did that horse kick me?"

"The horse had nothing to do with it," Elwyn said. "He's probably confused about why you brought him here to shoe and then went to sleep."

"What about my head?" he asked, rubbing his bruised temple.

"You must have hit your head on the anvil as you fell. You're lucky it seems to have been merely a glancing blow. Now, we need to get you to bed. You'll need rest to recover."

"I told you!" his wife said, her voice shaking. "I told you that you needed to ease up. You're too old for this kind of work."

"This isn't just about work," Elwyn said. "There are a number of factors involved. But rest is what's needed now."

Elwyn and Bryn together were able to lift the smith and half carry him into the house. Fortunately, the bedroom was on the ground floor, so they didn't have to get him up the stairs. They got him into bed, propped up on pillows. Elwyn made a cup of willow bark tea, which his wife fed to him, sip by sip, berating him the whole time.

While they did that, Elwyn pulled Bryn aside. "I know we need to go, but I'm afraid to leave him right now. I should watch him for at least an hour or two, and I'd like to give him one more dose, but that will need to wait."

"That's up to you. You're the one in the most danger."

She glanced back toward her patient and heaved a sigh. "They've been the worst to me, but it is my duty."

"So you've decided to trust yourself again?"

"I have. I do have a gift, and I should use it. Which

makes it all the more important that I get matters settled. But to do that, I would have to leave my patient."

"I'd say you should be able to linger for an hour. They shouldn't be able to get here any sooner than that. We don't even know that they're coming today. Then we'll get off the road as soon as we leave the village."

She nodded and returned to her patient, checking his pulse and opening her senses again to check his heart. Its beat was a little weak and irregular. One more dose should stabilize him better, but she'd prefer to wait so she wouldn't risk an overdose. While she waited, she sent Bryn back to the cottage to get the ingredients needed for ongoing treatment. She could leave those with the wife, who was sure to administer them as instructed.

Bryn returned half an hour later with several jars that he'd labeled. He wrote out Elwyn's instructions, and she repeated those to Sara to make sure she understood. "Rest is most important, though," she added. "No swinging a hammer or pumping bellows. I should be back in a week or so, and then we can see how you're progressing."

"I told you we needed to take on an apprentice," the wife said to her husband.

"And who in this village would I take on?" he asked. "There are no young men."

"We'll advertise with the next peddler who comes along. He can spread the word to other villages. There's got to be someone who wants to train as a smith or who wants to take over a forge. It's a good living."

"Not in this village," he said with a snort. "We don't have enough work to keep a new smith busy."

Elwyn cleared her throat. "Part of rest is staying calm," she said. "No excitement. No shouting or arguing."

"Tell her that," the smith muttered.

"I am. Now, one more dose of this medicine, and then I really must go." She administered one drop, then sat and monitored the smith's condition for a few more minutes until she was certain the dose wasn't too much. His heartbeat was much more regular. It looked like he'd made it through this crisis. If he followed her instructions, he might get somewhat better in time, but he was old and probably wouldn't fully recover.

Sara sent them off with some meat pies for their journey, and they hurried down the lane. It was far later than Elwyn had wanted to leave, but she had to hope it still wasn't too late.

When they neared the market square, her hopes were dashed. It was full of armed men on horseback, and in the middle of them was the baron—with the duke at his side.

CHAPTER 17

Elwyn grabbed Bryn's arm and pulled him to the side of the lane, up against a house so covered with wisteria that they could hide behind the vines. "They're already here," she said, despair welling up in her.

"They are?" he asked, moving to look beyond the vines before she pulled him back. "They must have had an early start and made it farther than I expected." He groaned. "I should have told you sooner. We could have left yesterday."

"But then the smith would have died."

She couldn't resist studying Maxen through the vines. Sunlight glinted off his golden hair and his armor as he sat tall in the saddle, an imposing figure. She waited for a pang of yearning to strike her upon seeing him again, but she mostly just felt angry. How did he feel about her? He was here, but did that mean he was eager to run a fugitive to ground, or did he merely want to find her?

If he'd wanted to find her, he wouldn't have brought her accuser, she decided. He was hunting a fugitive. He might have felt as betrayed as she did if he believed she'd used her position to murder a man under his command while under his roof, but then he could only feel that way because he'd assumed the worst about her. His betrayal was by far the worst. Her betrayal was only in his mind.

"They haven't seen us yet," Bryn said. "What do you want to do?"

"There's no point in heading to court if the duke's here."

"The duke's here?"

"The golden-haired one on the golden horse with the light mane."

"He matched his horse to his hair?"

She looked at the duke again. The horse was perfectly coordinated with him. How had she never noticed that? "I suppose he did, but I never thought he was particularly vain. He may not have done it on purpose."

"You're defending him?"

"I'm trying to be fair. If I can't be fair to him, I can't expect him to be fair to me."

"Murder and vanity are hardly on the same level when it comes to unfair accusations. Maybe he saved you a journey. You could talk to him here and see if you can get him to listen."

"I doubt that will do any good while the baron's here. He'll do everything he can to stop the duke from listening to me. I wouldn't be surprised if he tried to strike me down as a dangerous fugitive before I had a chance to speak. The plan was to go to the duke while Baron Vaughn was likely to be here and I could get the duke's ear without his influence. If the baron was able to persuade the duke to come here, I may not be able to get the duke to see reason. He's already made up his mind."

"To get out of the village, we'll have to go through the

market square. Do you think we could blend in with the market crowd and slip past?"

She didn't look at all like the elegant woman she'd been at court in her sturdy peasant clothes and with a straw hat shading her face, but she didn't want to risk it. "There's not much of a market crowd to blend in with, and it looks like they're investigating any woman who passes. But that's not the only way out. We could head up to the castle, and there's a walking path leading down from there that meets the lane near my cottage. That's how I thought you came to be in my garden when my theory was that you might have been held prisoner in the castle and had escaped."

"That's a good idea—going by the castle, not that I was a prisoner. At worst, I imagine the castle offers a lot of hiding places. You're sure it's abandoned?"

"Everyone here believes it is. The danger would be if the visiting nobles decide to stay there while they search for me. It's better for us to get out of here. I'm just concerned they would have left a guard by the cottage, so we'll have to be careful in that area."

"They didn't know about the cottage. We only knew that you were in the vicinity of the village."

"It's the healer's cottage, and I'm a healer, so it's pretty obvious."

"Would any of these nobles know what a healer's cottage even is?"

"Possibly not. But we'll be careful anyway. They may have posted a guard on the lane to watch for anyone leaving the village in that direction, so we'll have to stick to the woods."

They turned and headed back the way they'd come, up the lane that wound around a hill on the way to the castle, sticking to the shadows near the buildings so they wouldn't be visible from the market. "Where should we go if going to court would do no good?" Bryn asked.

"I don't know. Just somewhere not here until we figure something out. Eventually, whatever belongings of mine they have should lose their traces of me so it will be harder for them to find me. How long might that take?"

"That depends on the power of the wizard, but if Baron Vaughn went to my master, then he had to be desperate or dishonest enough that no other wizards would deal with him. My master was the wizard of last resort, the one willing to take jobs more ethical ones wouldn't." He shook his head. "I don't know why I stayed with him for so long, other than the fact that I had nowhere else to go and was useless at any other way of earning a living."

"Maybe I could look for another opportunity to approach the duke, when the baron isn't around," she mused aloud, trying to fight off the misgivings that grew larger with each step. "I would like to clear my name eventually." After a few more steps, she added, "I feel bad about promising Gladys that I'd come back."

"Maybe if they don't find you here, they'll leave."

"I wouldn't—" A scream from the market square cut her off. She turned back to see some of the soldiers grabbing a woman. Elwyn couldn't tell from this distance, but she thought it might have been Hana.

Mair's voice carried as she bellowed, "Leave her alone. What kind of man are you, letting your men abuse an innocent woman like that?"

Elwyn stopped in her tracks. They weren't going to give up, she knew, and other people would only be hurt if she left. She'd never be able to stop and rest, never be able to find a home and community again. She liked this home, this village, and she wasn't going to let them take it away from her. If the village had drawn her here for a reason, she was sure it would protect her and allow her to stay. It might even be for the best that things had happened this way. If she'd confronted the duke at his court, they would have been in his territory, surrounded by his people. But this was her village. He was the outsider here. These were her people. She'd served tea or prescribed herbs to almost everyone in the marketplace.

"I can't leave," she said with a heavy sigh. "I should face them now and get this over with. I'm tired of running. You can go, though. The baron won't be happy with you about getting in his way and using that memory spell."

He took her hand. "I'll stand with you, whatever you choose. It's my fault that they're here, and I don't want to run, either." He squeezed her hand, and she was surprised by how much stronger that made her feel.

She returned the squeeze. "Then let's go."

As they turned around and headed down the hill to the market, she began to have second thoughts. While she was sure most of the villagers would side with her, there weren't that many of them. The soldiers nearly outnumbered the entire village, and they did outnumber the people in the market. They were also armed and trained in using their weapons, and most of them would have no qualms about striking down people they regarded as peasants. The villagers would be armed only with tools and perhaps an angry chicken, and she wasn't sure how many of them would be willing to stand up to knights and lords, even if they'd shrugged off the disappearance of their own lord.

She also dreaded airing all her woes in the market square, surrounded by her friends, neighbors, customers, and patients. All the details of her past were likely to come out, and she didn't know what they'd think of her in the aftermath. She might have to move on even if she wasn't arrested. She was glad she'd told Bryn everything. At least he wouldn't be shocked by anything that was said. Well, almost everything. She'd told him about the murder accusation, but not the extent of her relationship with the duke. That made this whole affair even more sordid.

When they reached the market square, she kept her head down and tried to walk like a weary peasant, blending in among the other villagers. As long as the nobles didn't recognize her, she had the upper hand. She could move among them and position herself perfectly for this confrontation, as long as no villager greeted her by name.

The soldiers were still hassling Hana. Mair berated them for accosting the weaver, and none of them so much as looked at Elwyn. She wasn't sure whether to be flattered or insulted. Based on the questions they shouted at the villagers, she got the impression the soldiers were looking for someone a lot more elegant than she currently appeared, so they must have thought she was impressive in her days at court, and they didn't see that woman in her current appearance. They focused their questions on Hana, probably because she looked weak and frail. Little did they know what the woman had survived already. They wouldn't break her.

In fact, she was standing up to them quite boldly, much to Elwyn's surprise. "How dare you lay hands on me!" she snapped, wrenching herself out of a soldier's grasp. "I have nothing to do with the woman you seek." It seemed adversity truly brought out her inner strength. Elwyn wanted to applaud her.

"Leave her be," the duke said. "I don't think she's here."

"The peddler said there was a woman selling herbs who fit her description," the baron said, looking around the market. Elwyn ducked her head so that her hat brim shielded her face.

A peddler? So, it wasn't Bryn's spell breaking that told them where she was. It must have been the peddler who'd accosted her who'd reported her. She still would have been able to leave earlier if Bryn had told her what he knew sooner, but it wasn't entirely his fault that the baron had found the village.

Elwyn passed the baron, holding her breath and hoping he didn't recognize her until she'd had a chance to talk to Duke Maxen. She got as close as she could to the duke and looked up at him on his horse. He still had a golden glow about him, but from this close she could see the strands of silver at his temples and the lines at the corners of his eyes. Had he aged that much in her absence, or had she been as blind to his physical faults as she had been to the truth about their relationship?

He still hadn't recognized her, even as she passed right by him. She had probably aged more since she last saw him than he had, given that she'd spent much of that time starving, walking, and sleeping outdoors. When she had Maxen between her and the baron and the baron was looking elsewhere, she took off her hat and called to the duke, "Did you come here looking for me?"

He turned toward her, color draining from his face in shock. "Elwyn?" he said.

"Yes. It's me. And I have something to say to you. I did not kill Sir Aled, either deliberately or accidentally. If you knew me at all, you would know that to be true, and the fact that you were ever even the least bit willing to consider that tells me that you are not the man I thought you were."

He looked like she'd just slapped him, but he didn't get

a chance to respond before the baron shouted, "There she is! Seize her!"

Maxen had yet another chance to stand up for her as there was time for him to call off the soldiers while they rushed toward her, but he didn't say anything, whether because he was still stunned or because he agreed with the order, she couldn't tell. It was Bryn who drew his sword and blocked the way. "Keep your hands off her," he snapped, brandishing the sword. She wasn't sure if he could actually do anything with the sword, but he didn't look entirely incompetent. The soldiers actually held back.

The baron laughed. "You're going to do what, foolish wizard? You're as useless with a sword as you are with a spell."

"How long did you go without regaining your memory?" Bryn asked. "I'd say that wasn't useless."

"I didn't lose my memory. I only forgot about coming here, and that spell broke as soon as I arrived."

Elwyn couldn't see Bryn's face to see how he reacted to that news, but he did hesitate before replying, "It didn't matter then, did it?" If he'd wiped his own memory, down to his identity, while his target had merely forgotten where he'd gone and why, then perhaps he wasn't wrong about being the worst wizard ever. Or she'd been right about him wanting to forget himself, and that had enhanced the spell.

"Take her!" the baron ordered his men, but finally Maxen held up a hand to stop them. They looked between the duke and the baron, uncertain which order to follow.

"There's no need to grab her," Maxen said. "She's not going anywhere."

By this time, the other villagers had noticed the confrontation and had come over to see what was happening. "Wyn, what is this?" Mair called out from beyond the soldiers who'd circled Elwyn.

"These people are the reason I ended up here," Elwyn explained.

Mair looked up at the duke, then back at Elwyn with a wry smile. "Ah, so he's the louse who didn't stand up for you." Elwyn had to fight her own smile. Only Mair would be so bold as to insult a duke to his face.

"Elwyn Howell, I arrest you for the murder of Sir Aled," the baron said, forcing his horse through the circle of soldiers.

"How are you sure that I murdered him?" Elwyn asked him. "I had no contact with him between the time I tended him and the time you announced his death."

His face red with rage, he shook an accusing finger at her. "You let him die on purpose."

"He wasn't injured that badly. That wasn't a fatal wound. I could have left him totally alone without doing anything to treat his wound, and he would have lived. His death had nothing to do with me." Knowing she was taking a huge risk, she walked straight to his horse, pausing to give Bryn a look that she hoped signaled to him that she didn't need him rushing to her defense, and held up her hands, wrists together, as though offering herself to be bound. "If you're arresting me, do so yourself."

Anyone with half a brain would have expected a trap, but he swung himself out of the saddle and approached her gleefully. "It would be my honor," he said with a sneer, reaching out to grab her hands.

In that moment, she made the connection. She couldn't read his direct thoughts, but when she plunged into his consciousness at the depth she went, she could come close. She almost never went that deep because it wasn't necessary for her work and it was intrusive, but if there was ever a time to use her gift to its fullest extent, this was it. "Guilt," she said. "Regret. A good man lost, but it had to be done, the best opportunity. Clear the way of obstacles."

The baron released her abruptly. "Take her!" he called to his men, who grabbed her. To the duke, he said, "She lies, of course. She always was ambitious. That's why she wormed her way in so close to you."

That wasn't the way it had gone at all, but if Maxen didn't realize it, she doubted anything she said would matter. The duke did look somewhat torn, though, like he was having second thoughts. "If you didn't let him die, then how did he die?" he asked Elwyn.

"You should ask the one who feels guilty about his death," she replied.

"Why would he kill his own man?"

"Yes, why would I kill my own man?" the baron asked. "On the other hand, I know you never liked him."

"But what would I have gained from letting him die? The only possible reason would be to spend less time patching up serving girls who got in his way and making sure they wouldn't have to suffer any other consequences from his actions."

"So it was revenge!" the baron shouted. "You heard her. That's a confession."

"Quite the opposite," she said. "It sounds like you're the one who's desperate to pin the killing on someone so no one will look for the real killer." She looked up at Maxen. "Do you really think I would kill someone or even allow someone to die, merely because I didn't like him?" She met his gaze and held it, forcing him to look at her, *really* look at her, as he considered. She thought he looked torn. Or perhaps confused. A thought struck her—the baron had to have had a potion or poison to kill the knight, and he'd hired a wizard to track her down. Had he also used magic to cloud Maxen's mind?

"Of course she didn't!" a voice called out. Sara Smith approached, her market basket over her arm. To Elwyn, she added, "So, this is why you were in such a hurry this morning."

"What is this?" Maxen demanded.

Sara glared up at him. "She would have made it well out of the village before you arrived, but I came to her in need of help. My husband had taken ill. Instead of escaping, she came to his aid. Even after she saved him, she probably could have left and made it safely away before you got here, but she waited to be sure he wouldn't take another bad turn, and she took the time to give me the medicines I'd need to treat him. She sacrificed her freedom for us, and she has no reason to care about us. We've made her life miserable since she got here. We've tried to drive her away. Her life would have been easier without us. So, if she would risk everything to help people who've been awful to her, why would she kill someone she didn't like when she had nothing really to gain from it?"

Elwyn had to blink rapidly to keep the tears that had come to her eyes from falling. Sara was the last person she would have expected to come to her defense, and that made her defense all the more effective. The question was, would it work?

CHAPTER 18

For a moment, Elwyn thought Maxen might see reason. The cloud that seemed to cover his features cleared, and he turned toward the baron, but then he swayed slightly in the saddle and turned back to Elwyn. "That is no evidence," he said coldly.

"He has you under a spell, doesn't he?" Elwyn accused, saying it more for Bryn's benefit than to get the duke to think. Bryn might be an incompetent wizard—or thought he was—but maybe he could break a spell if he tried. If the magic came from his master, he might be familiar with it. Hoping he picked up on what she needed him to do, she added, "He's admitted he worked with a wizard to find me. Maybe he got the potion that killed Sir Aled from a wizard, and that might explain your disloyalty to me."

"But why would Vaughn bother?" Maxen asked. "You asked what you had to gain by killing Aled, but he has even less to gain from killing his own man."

She had an idea, but it would mean airing the full extent of her relationship with Maxen. They'd been discreet, so it hadn't been general knowledge at court. Most people knew only that she had his ear and that he trusted her counsel. She hadn't told anyone in the village, not even Mair or Bryn, that they had been lovers. Mair had probably assumed, since that was how her mind worked, but she hated to think of how Bryn would take it. It had happened before they met, and she and Bryn were not involved romantically, beyond some feelings and that one kiss, but she still felt odd about him finding out, especially this way.

She faced the baron. "You have a sister, don't you? And you had plans for her. You wanted to make her a duchess, and then you'd be connected to the duke in a way that would ensure your rise. But that would only work if the duke became lonely enough to seek companionship. That meant getting his closest companion out of the way—not just eliminated, but discredited, so his heart wouldn't go with her."

"You're lying, making things up," the baron said, but she ignored him, turning to watch the duke instead. He'd frozen completely.

"That is what happened," Maxen said, frowning. "Soon after you left, his sister came to court, and she began spending time with me. We were to be married at the next full moon." Turning to the baron with a frown, he asked, "Did you arrange that?"

"It takes no arranging for my sister to visit me at court," the baron insisted.

While the duke and the baron were distracted, Elwyn glanced toward Bryn. He was mumbling under his breath and frantically wiggling his fingers. She hoped he was working on a spell, and she hoped it didn't do something horrible to everyone in the market.

"You love my sister," the baron said, stressing every word. Elwyn noticed that as he spoke he placed his hand on a pouch that hung at his belt. Maxen's expression clouded again. She was now certain Vaughn was using magic.

"Bryn!" she called out, catching his gaze and directing it to the baron's waist.

At the same time, the baron shoved his men aside and grabbed her, holding his sword across her throat. It appeared that he didn't plan to take any chances that he might lose his influence over the duke. "She lies!" he shouted. "She's the one who had you under her malign influence, ever since she came to your court. She snared you in her web of seduction from the very beginning. In fact, are you certain that she wasn't the one who caused your children's illness, so that she'd have an excuse to spend time with you and get you under her spell?

The children's illness had been the reason Elwyn was brought to court in the first place, and they'd been ill before Elwyn ever met the duke, so it would have been impossible for her to be responsible. Unfortunately, she wasn't sure Maxen would be able to recall this while he was under Vaughn's enchantment, and she didn't dare speak with the baron's blade at her throat.

She caught a glint of sunlight on metal out of the corner of her eye, and the next thing she saw was Bryn rushing toward her, his sword out. She groaned inwardly. Although she appreciated the effort, he didn't stand a chance against the baron and his men. His blade flashed through the air and slashed somewhere on the baron's right side. The baron couldn't block the blow while holding Elwyn, and the soldiers didn't seem to know what to do. Bryn backed away out of their reach before they could react.

The baron made no sound of pain and didn't loosen his hold on Elwyn. Bryn must have missed him somehow. She heard a soft thud, then something slid across the ground, landing at Bryn's feet, as though someone behind the baron had kicked it. Bryn bent to pick it up. It was the pouch that had been on the baron's belt. Bryn must have picked up on her cue and cut it off. When he opened it, a small stone fell out of it into his hand.

"Aha!" he said. "I recognize this." He mumbled something over the stone, and Maxen's expression cleared.

"What is this?" the duke demanded.

"He had you enchanted to influence you, your grace," Bryn said. "This is my master's work. I know my master worked with him to find Elwyn, and I'll wager he had something to do with the potion that killed your knight."

"Seize him!" the duke shouted to the soldiers, pointing at the baron.

"He lies!" the baron insisted, tightening his grip on Elwyn. She felt the edge of his blade digging into her throat. "That rock is no charm. It's merely something I carry for luck."

"Then why do I feel so different now that you no longer have it? And why do you feel the need for a hostage? Release her and let's discuss this like men."

That was a definite change. Elwyn felt some relief that Maxen hadn't really betrayed her, after all. He'd been under a spell, so he wasn't himself. Now he was standing up for her.

"Call off your men," the baron ordered. "I will kill her."

"What outcome do you expect from this?" the duke asked. "You've been accused of murder. I have evidence that you were magically influencing me. Whatever you hoped to achieve, it will not happen. I will not be marrying your sister. You will stand trial and be stripped of your title and lands. Killing Elwyn will only add to your crimes. There will be no benefit to you. If you strike her down, you will be killed on the spot."

"But the witch will die with me."

Elwyn wasn't sure how she was going to get out of this. Vaughn knew he was trapped, and he was just mean enough to want to take her with him, since he blamed her for his plan's failure, just as he'd blamed her for his inability to get the influence over the duke that he'd wanted.

Maybe Bryn could do something magical, she hoped, trying to catch his eye. Did he have enough confidence in his power to wield it in a crisis? She'd even be willing to risk losing a bit of her memory if he could save her life.

It was funny, but in this moment she had the strongest sense of clarity she'd ever felt. She knew exactly what she wanted out of life, where she wanted to be, and with whom. She loved this crazy little village. She wanted to be able to make it thrive again—not so much that it lost its character, but enough for the people to be able to make a living there. She wanted there to be families and children, a bustling market, and plenty of festivals, maybe even a lord in the castle. She wanted to keep the village healthy. She wanted people gathered in her tea shop, chatting about their lives and their plans. She wanted to be part of that.

She even thought she might want Bryn. She'd fallen in love with the man he was when he didn't know who he was. She was a little less certain now. She'd need to take time to get to know him as he really was, just as she suspected he needed some time to figure out who he was. But there was definitely potential there, and her feelings for him hadn't completely gone away when his memories returned. It was a different feeling than she'd ever had with the duke, something deeper and truer, and she felt like he saw her in a way the duke never had.

But she wouldn't be able to have any of these things she wanted if she didn't survive this incident. If the village had brought her here, it was time for it to step up and do something to keep her here.

A loud squawk pierced the air, along with a flapping, fluttering sound, and suddenly the sword dropped away from her throat. She took advantage of the opportunity to jump away from the baron's grasp and turned to see him flailing at the very angry chicken that had perched on his head and was trying to peck at his eyes. "Get it off! Get it off!" he shouted.

The soldiers looked to the duke for guidance, but the duke acted as though he didn't see anything. Elwyn thought she detected a trace of amusement on his face. She turned back to the baron to see Lucina running up behind him, her largest rolling pin held up like a club. "I'll get it for you!" she cried. The chicken fluttered away at the last second, and she hit the baron square on the head with the rolling pin. He crumpled to the ground. "Oops, missed," she said with a sly grin.

Meanwhile, Mair and Bryn rushed to Elwyn's side. Bryn held his sword, as though daring any soldiers to come near. Mair just glared at them, which may have been even more frightening. When she winked at one guard, he darted behind one of his colleagues, cowering in fear. Other villagers surrounded Elwyn, blocking the soldiers from getting close to her. Even Sara Smith joined them. Tears stung Elwyn's eyes at the show of support. The village had come to her rescue—not the village itself or whatever mystical entity lay behind it, but the people of the village, which was even more important to her. She blinked away the tears so she wouldn't be seen crying, but she wanted to hug all of them, even the smith's wife and the Chicken Lady.

"Mistress Elwyn is cleared of all charges," the duke said, his voice ringing over the marketplace. "If Baron Vaughn lives, he is charged with murder, undue magical influence, and probably several more offenses. Due to his actions today, in full view of witnesses, he is stripped of his rank, title, and lands, regardless of the outcome of any trial for the murder of Sir Aled." The villagers cheered, and Mair hugged Elwyn.

The soldiers all appeared visibly relieved. They lowered their weapons, and their shoulders relaxed. Elwyn couldn't help but wonder if they'd actually liked Vaughn and believed in him or if they'd merely been following orders. Either way, they didn't seem to be a threat to her anymore.

She wanted to celebrate, but first she had a patient to see to. She went to kneel next to Vaughn. His face had been scratched by the chicken's talons, but she was more concerned about the blow from Lucina's rolling pin. It wasn't so much that she worried about how it had affected him, since he was likely heading for the gallows, but she didn't want Lucina to feel responsible for having seriously harmed someone. It might have felt good for her to have had the opportunity to take action instead of feeling help-less the way nightmares often made a person feel, but Elwyn didn't think that guilt would help her.

"You're going to tend his injuries after everything that he's done?" Maxen asked, sounding incredulous

She turned to look up at him. "Did you not hear anything that anyone said here? I have a duty to tend to everyone in need of help, regardless of who they are or how I feel about them. I didn't let Sir Aled die, and I won't let him die, either, no matter what he did to me."

She placed her hand on Vaughn's forehead and opened her senses. She felt the sting of the wounds on his face and scalp. The rolling pin had mostly stunned him. He'd have a lump on the back of his head, but she didn't find any bleeding or swelling under the skull. He wasn't unconscious, merely dazed and humiliated. Blinking out of the connection, she said, "I don't think there will be any long-term harm to him. He won't feel good, but he shouldn't be impaired." She opened her bag and dabbed salve on the wounds from the chicken's feet and applied a tincture to reduce bruising to the lump on his head. She could tell from his responses that he was awake enough to feel the sting of the salve on his wounds.

It was only after she'd put away her supplies that she realized she'd now fully demonstrated her abilities to the village. True, she'd treated the Chicken Lady at the festival, but that had been less obvious. Today, she'd shown that he did have the power of empathy. She'd never be just an herbalist to the villagers again—if she ever had been nothing more than that. They'd looked to her as a healer from the very beginning, she realized. Gladys letting her stay in the cottage had been an obvious sign to those who knew about the helper.

"Will he be able to travel today?" the duke asked.

Vaughn groaned and sat up, holding his head. "Ask him," she said.

"I just want to get away from here," Vaughn said with a groan.

"Is there a place my men can water their horses and refresh themselves?" the duke asked.

"You can go to the inn's stableyard," Mair said, pointing. "The inn's closed, but there's still a pump with fresh water."

The duke glanced at the sky, then turned to one of his men. "We leave when the sun is at zenith. Have the men water the horses and get whatever else they need. Any food they want must be paid for. We should be able to make it back to where we spent last night. See to my horse." The soldier nodded and went to convey the information to the other soldiers.

When they were gone, the duke returned his attention to Elwyn. He dismounted, handed his reins over to the nearest soldier, and rushed to Elwyn to take her hands in his. "Can you forgive me?" he asked. "I can only imagine what you must have thought when I took Vaughn's side and never defended you."

"It wasn't your fault," she said, fighting to ignore the faces Mair was making from behind the duke.

"Was that why you fled, because you didn't believe I would protect you or ensure you got justice? You should have known I would never abandon you like that."

That took her aback. She slid her hands out of his grasp and stepped away, putting more distance between them. "How should I have known that you'd protect me?" she asked. "You didn't say anything to defend me, even when I asked you to. I had no choice but to flee. I couldn't risk my life on you suddenly speaking out when you hadn't already." Having been away from him and having a different kind of relationship for comparison had shown her that although they'd been friends, their relationship hadn't been that deep. He'd come to her for comfort and companionship, but now that she thought about it, he'd never cared that much about her. It was all about what he needed from her.

"But you can come back to court now," he said. "Your name will be cleared." He reached to brush a stray strand of hair from her face. "I've missed you so much." He moved toward her and bent to kiss her, but she moved away from him again.

"No, I don't think I can go back to court," she said. "I'm not the same person I was then. A lot has happened since I left. I've rediscovered my calling, and I can do more good here than I ever could at court, among people who truly need me."

He looked around at the tiny, mostly empty village. She supposed that through his eyes it wasn't much, but she saw something entirely different. She saw a community—Mair and Lucina, the Chicken Lady, the miller and his wife, even Sara—and every one of them was worth more than all the nobles in court combined.

She unfastened the chain that hung around her neck and removed the necklace from under her blouse. "I should give this back to you. I'm not part of your court anymore."

She handed it to him, but he closed his fist so she couldn't place it in his palm. "Keep it. Melt it down for the gold if you want. I owe you that much, since I took so much away from you." He reached to take her hand and added softly, "I can't persuade you to come back? I have missed you."

For a moment, she opened her senses to feel what he was feeling. He did miss her, and in a way that made her shiver, but the person he wanted wasn't who she was now. "I can't go back to that life," she said, sliding her hand out of his grasp. "No matter what's said about my innocence, I don't think I'll be fully accepted there. He poisoned too many people against me. There may even be those who blame me for him being accused. You know that."

With a sigh, he said, "I do. And it's likely to be worse since I'll have to break that engagement."

"I take it she wouldn't have been your choice if you hadn't been enchanted."

"You know that I have no plans to remarry. And not to her. Did you ever meet her?"

Elwyn shook her head. "No. I wasn't really part of the court, so I wouldn't have met her unless I saw her as a patient."

He studied her for a long moment, awareness gradually dawning in his eyes. "I imagine you were lonely there. You didn't fit in with anyone."

"That was why I was glad of your friendship."

"But not enough to come back."

"No. I learned a lot about myself after I left court. There's something about losing everything that shows you who you really are. I belong here, doing this kind of work. I can't explain it, but I have the strongest feeling I was meant to be here, that I have a purpose to fulfill."

He frowned and looked around at the village. "What do you do in a place like this?"

"I help people," she said with a shrug. "I tend to wounds and illnesses. I sell the herbs they need. And I run a little tea shop where people meet to have tea and talk. It's nice." His skeptical expression only made her laugh.

"You run a tea shop?"

Mair joined her and hooked her elbow through Elwyn's, creating a chain of support. "The tea shop is the heart of our community. I'm afraid we can't let her go."

He nodded. "You're always welcome at my court if you change your mind. Be well, Elwyn." He turned to see that his men were coming out of the inn's stableyard with their horses. He gave her the slightest bow before turning and heading toward his horse.

"So, you're staying?" Mair said, then hugged Elwyn. As

soon as that hug ended, she was caught up in Bryn's arms, then Lucina hugged her, nearly taking her breath away. The other villagers joined in, cheering.

Then she found herself facing Sara. "I'm grateful for what you do, though you're still wasting time with that trivial tea shop, and you're a strumpet living with that man in your house."

Elwyn was so taken aback by what Sara said that she couldn't react until the woman had turned to walk away, and then she couldn't help but laugh. Her friends joined in, and she had to wipe tears from the corners of her eyes, though she wasn't sure if they were from the laughter or were from all the other emotions coming out in the aftermath of her ordeal.

"Everyone, mount up!" the duke called. "Take Vaughn. And the wizard is also coming with us."

CHAPTER 19

"What?" Elwyn cried out as horror replaced joy. "You can't take him!"

"I need him to give evidence against Vaughn," the duke explained.

Bryn nodded, then said, "He's right. I need to go. I can testify that Vaughn was planning to kill you, not arrest you, and I may even be able to show that he had my master make the potion that killed the knight. I need to do this."

He took both her hands and looked her in the eyes. "I will be back." With a smile, he added, "And I need to formally resign my apprenticeship. It'll also be good to pick up my own clothes." He glanced ruefully down at his ill-fitting attire.

She reluctantly released his hands. "Then go and be well, but come back as soon as you can." The soldiers gave him the baron's horse. Elwyn noted that he seemed to know how to ride. He didn't look quite as strong in the saddle as the soldiers did, but he didn't look as awkward as he did with a sword.

It was with decidedly mixed emotions that she watched

the duke and his men ride out of the marketplace. There was a great sense of relief at no longer being a fugitive, but she hated to see Bryn go just as she was getting to see who he really was.

"If one of you wants to be a smith, there's an apprenticeship open at the forge!" Sara shouted after the departing soldiers.

Mair draped an arm around Elwyn. "He'll be back," she assured Elwyn.

"Of course he will," the Chicken Lady said. "The village wants him here, just as it wasn't ready to let you go." She wandered off, surrounded by chickens.

"It's a little alarming how comforting I found that," Elwyn remarked. Now that everything was over, she felt shaky and weak. She wasn't sure her legs would get her home.

"I feel like I missed something somewhere," Mair said. "Bryn's a wizard? I take it that means he got his memories back."

"During the festival. And he's an apprentice wizard, though he claims he's not a very good one. He did manage to break the spell on the duke, so maybe he's better than he realizes."

"But what about the important thing: Does he have a wife?"

"No wife."

"Well, that's good. Come on, I'll give you a ride home." She guided Elwyn toward her cart.

"I'll be by soon with some tarts," Lucina said.

"Yes, some sweets would be good after all that excitement," Elwyn said, treating herself like a patient. She climbed onto the back of the cart. Mair got onto the driver's seat and clicked her tongue to get the horse going.

Sitting on the back of the cart, Elwyn watched the village pass by. "This really is a pretty village, isn't it?" she remarked.

"I suppose so," Mair said.

"No, really, I traveled through a lot of places on the way here, and this was the most beautiful place. That's why it's so strange that it's so empty. You'd think people would be flocking here."

"I think the village can afford to be choosy. It only selects certain people to live here. You're fortunate you made the cut."

"I am. And I'm lucky it wanted me to stay." She shuddered at the thought of how things could have gone if the village hadn't been on her side.

"*We* wanted you to stay." Mair pulled up in front of the cottage, got down from the cart and tied her horse to the fence while Elwyn managed to get down from the cart in spite of feeling so shaky. Mair offered her an arm to lean on as they made their way to the front door.

"Gladys, I'm back!" Elwyn called out as they entered.

"Gladys?" Mair asked.

"That's what I call the helper. You do know about the helper, don't you? You hinted that you did."

"Yes, but I didn't know she had a name."

"That was the name of the first healer to live here. I think her influence has remained."

By the time they made it to the kitchen, Gladys had already put on a kettle. Either she'd kept the fire going, or her magic allowed one to start instantly. "Stay for lunch," Elwyn urged Mair. "Sara gave me a meat pie for the journey, and I might as well share it with you." She got it out of her bag and put it on the table. It soon flew into a pot that was hung over the fire.

"Let me get my cart home and unloaded, and I'll be back by the time it's warm," Mair said.

After Mair left, Elwyn gave Gladys a quick summary of everything that had happened while the helper brewed tea and added plenty of honey to it. "So, it looks like I'm here to stay," Elwyn concluded. "I don't know when Bryn will be back. I'm sure he will be."

Mair returned with some cheese and cream. "It looks like one of the soldiers took Sara up on that apprenticeship offer. He'd turned back when I went out to the cart, and he asked for directions to the forge. Now, I need to know all the details about that duke," she said as they sat down to lunch. "I'm glad you chose to stay with us, but you really chose us over a duke?"

"I wouldn't actually have had a duke. That was the problem. It's complicated, but I was mostly someone convenient he wouldn't have to marry, but who he could treat as almost an equal."

"At least he was only a rat because of magic."

"That is nice to know."

"I like Bryn better—or whoever he is. What do you know about him?"

Elwyn had just finished telling her the parts she thought Bryn wouldn't mind her sharing when Lucina arrived with berry tarts, which the three of them ate with cream. "I should probably open the shop," Elwyn said when she'd eaten the last morsel.

"You should rest," Mair said. "They'll all be curious, of course, but they also know you probably aren't up to much after all the excitement."

Elwyn did open the next day, though. The house was far too empty without Bryn in it, so she looked forward to having some company each day. She had to tell an edited version of the story to explain the events in the market to all the villagers who came by, full of curiosity. Now that she'd been open about being a healer, she found herself called upon more often. It was more than enough to keep her busy. She could barely keep her eyes open to read a little in the evenings, and she missed Bryn reading to her.

After a couple of weeks, she was starting to worry that he wouldn't be returning, after all, when she was working in the shop one afternoon and saw a small wagon pull up in front of the cottage. That was unusual. Her customers walked to the shop. Only Mair ever drove up in a cart, and only when she was coming back from the market or on her way somewhere else. Elwyn went to the front door to see who it was and was shocked to see Bryn, wearing clothes that actually fit him, coming up the walk with a box in his arms.

"You're back?" she said, not sure he was really there. She'd imagined his return so often that she wasn't sure this wasn't a dream.

He gave her a grin that looked so much like the way he'd been without his memories that she wondered if he'd lost his memories again. "I'm back, and I brought you some tea and other supplies. You never did make that shopping list for me, so I had to guess." He went past her to the counter, greeting the customers as though he'd only gone out to the shops. "I used the money you gave me for the journey, since I didn't need it," he added to Elwyn. "I hope you don't mind."

"No, not at all."

He set the box the counter, then headed for the door. "You're leaving again already?" Elwyn called out as she tried to catch up with him.

"Just getting the next load. I have your belongings. The

duke sent them. Do you want your books in the sitting room?"

"Yes, that would be lovely," she said, stunned. She followed him to the wagon, where he handed her a small crate and picked up one, himself, then they went back inside and to the sitting room, where he set down his crate and took her crate from her and set it down. Her emotions finally escaped the numbness of shock, and with a cry of joy, she threw her arms around him. "You're back! I missed you so much."

He responded by holding her tight enough that she could barely breathe, but she didn't mind. He eased his grasp slightly just before she started feeling lightheaded. "I take it this means you're not mad at me anymore."

"I can be mad and miss you and worry about you, all at the same time." Releasing him and stepping back slightly, but still staying in the circle of his arms, she asked, "What happened?"

"The baron—well, former baron—was stripped of his rank and convicted. It turned out he did get the potion from my master. Which means I'm now completely free of any apprenticeship obligation, as he was convicted, as well, which means he was kicked out of the wizards' guild." He released his hold on her and headed toward the door. "Now, we need to make another trip to the wagon. There's a trunk. The duke also sent all your clothes."

Elwyn had to laugh. "I'm not sure what good court clothes will do me here."

"Wear them to dinner. Such as dinner tonight."

"I don't have anything in the house worthy of that festive an occasion."

He grinned. "I do. Have dinner with me tonight at my place."

She felt like her wits hadn't yet caught up with her. Part of her wasn't entirely sure he was really back, and it was as though a different person had returned. He was closer to the person he'd been without his memories, but there was something somewhat more serious about him. "Your place?" she asked. "You're not staying here?"

"I decided to take over the inn, since no one else is using it. On the off chance that someone comes to town, I can offer rooms. Otherwise, I'll do a dinner or two a week for the villagers. And when I'm not cooking, I'll study and practice. I brought all my books. I have a feeling there may come a time when this village will need a wizard."

"Oh. You've clearly been doing some thinking."

"Quite a lot of it. I had time on the journey, and there was a lot of waiting around at court. And you're right, I need to figure out who I really am, but I can't hide from my past, either." He reached and took her hand. "Let's start over, like we're meeting for the first time, which we are, in a sense. I am Bryn, an innkeeper studying to be a wizard."

With a smile, she gave him a slight curtsy. "Pleased to meet you. I am Elwyn, a healer who also runs a tea shop."

He bowed. "Delighted to make your acquaintance. Elwyn, would you like to have dinner with me tonight at the inn?"

"Yes, I would," she said.

"Then we'd better bring in the rest of your things. You'll need something nice to wear."

It took the two of them to bring in the trunk and haul it upstairs. Before heading back down, he glanced at the room he'd used. "I hope you don't mind that I decided to live on my own. But I do need to figure out a lot of things, and I need to find my own calling."

"It'll keep Sara from calling me a strumpet. For that reason, at least."

He beamed at her, and it was like the sun coming out after a storm. "Good. Then dinner tonight? I'll come get you just before sunset, since the duke was also kind enough to provide me with a horse and wagon. I can offer rides to nearby towns if the inn doesn't keep me busy." He bowed and added, "I'm looking forward to making your acquaintance, my lady."

"And I'm looking forward to getting to know you, my good sir." More seriously, she added, "And I'm glad you came back."

"I don't think Rydding would have let me stay away."

≈

About the Author

SHANNA SWENDSON earned a journalism degree from the University of Texas and used to work in public relations but decided it was more fun to make up the people she wrote about, so now she's a full-time novelist. She lives in Irving, Texas, with several hardy houseplants and too many books to fit on the shelves.

Visit her web site and sign up for her mailing list at shannaswendson.com

Printed in Great Britain
by Amazon